Assigned Eighth Air Force: September 1942
Component Squadrons: 367th, 368th, and 444th
Bombardment Squadron (H)
Station: Bassingbourn, England. 7 December 1942 to
15 December 1945 (Air echelon arrived 8
through 14 September 1942
First Mission: 9 October 1942
Last Mission: 19 April 1945
Total Missions: 342
Total Credit Sorties: 9,614
Total Bomb Tonnage: 22,575 (248 tons of leaflets)
Aircraft Missing In Action: 171
Enemy Aircraft Claims: 332
Major Awards: One Medal of Honor (SSgt Richard
Jones — 1 May 1945)
Two Distinguishd Unit Citations
Five Legion of Merits
Twenty-two Silver Stars
Eight-hundred Distinguished Flying
Crosses
Sixty-five Bronze Stars
Five Soldier's Medals
Four hundred and one Purple Hearts
Personnel Casualities: Killed in Action: 483
Missing in Action: 305
Wounded in Action: 145
Prisoners of War: 884

FIRST-RATE ADVENTURES FOR MEN

SOLDIER FOR HIRE #1: ZULU BLOOD (777, $2.50)
by Robert Skimin
Killing is what J.C. Stonewall is paid for. And he'll do any job—for the right price. But when he gets caught in the middle of a bloody revolution in Zimbabwe, his instinct for survival is put to the ultimate test!

SOLDIER FOR HIRE #2: TROJAN IN IRAN (793, $2.50)
by Robert Skimin
Stonewall loathes Communists and terrorists, so he is particularly eager for his next assignment—in Iran! He joins forces with the anti-Ayatollah Kurds, and will stop at nothing to blow apart the Iranian government!

THE SURVIVALIST #1: TOTAL WAR (768, $2.25)
by Jerry Ahern
The first in the shocking series that follows the unrelenting search for ex-CIA covert operations officer John Thomas Rourke to locate his missing family—after the button is pressed, the missiles launched and the multimegaton bombs unleashed . . .

THE SURVIVALIST #2:
THE NIGHTMARE BEGINS (810, $2.50)
by Jerry Ahern
After WW III, the United States is just a memory. But ex-CIA covert operations office Rourke hasn't forgotten his family. While hiding from the Soviet occupation forces, he adheres to his search!

THE SURVIVALIST #3: THE QUEST (851, $2.50)
by Jerry Ahern
Not even a deadly game of intrigue within the Soviet High Command, the formation of the American "resistance" and a highly placed traitor in the new U.S. government can deter Rourke from continuing his desperate search for his family.

Available wherever paperbacks are sold, or order direct from the Publisher. Send cover price plus 50¢ per copy for mailing and handling to Zebra Books, 475 Park Avenue South, New York, N.Y. 10016. DO NOT SEND CASH!

IN SEARCH OF EAGLES

BY CHRISTOPHER SLOAN

ZEBRA BOOKS
KENSINGTON PUBLISHING CORP.

ZEBRA BOOKS

are published by

KENSINGTON PUBLISHING CORP.
475 Park Avenue South
New York, N.Y. 10016

For my children, Ali and Paul, for knowing how to love, and knowing how to laugh.

ACKNOWLEDGMENTS

With deep gratitude to Neal Ringvall, former First Lieutenant and B-17 navigator, who was there when it really happened. Between February and August 1944, Mr. Ringvall flew out of Thurleigh Airfield, England. During this time, he was awarded the Distinguished Flying Cross and the Air Medal for outstanding courage and airmanship. Mr. Ringvall flew with the 367th Bombardment Squadron (H), which was part of the 306th Air Group in the 8th Air Force. Numerous hours were spent listening to him recreate his experiences—told clearly and honestly. As I listened, I also learned the meaning of dedication and duty. Because of his patience and understanding, many of the scenes in this book came to life. More importantly, I gained a friend.

Grateful acknowledgment is made to the following for permission to reprint previously published son lyrics:

Chapel & Co., Inc., for *I Can't Get Started,* by Ira Gershwin and Vernon Duke, Copyright © 1935 by Chappel & Co., Inc., International Copyright Secured, All Rights Reserved, Used by Permission. Chappel & Co., Inc., for *The Lady Is A Tramp*, by Rodgers and Hart Copyright © 1937 by Chappel & Co., Inc., International Copyright Secured, All Rights Reserved, Used By Permission. Hoffman Songs Inc., Hallmark Music Co. Inc., & Drake Activities Corp., for *Mairzy Doats,* Copyright © 1943, © Copyright renewed 1971, Used by Permission. *Blues In the Night*, by Johnny Mercer & Harold Arlen, © 1941 (Renewed) Warner Brothers, Inc., All Rights Reserved, Used by Permission.

Everyone wants to get to heaven, but no one wants to die.

> —Joe Louis
> Heavyweight Champion of the World

We are the most destructive men in the history of mankind. We destroy and that is our work, and I love it.

> —SSgt Benito "Benny" Tutone
> Flight Engineer/Turret Gunner
> 45th Bombardment Group (H)
> Bassingbourn, England

I call it murder.

> —Captain James L. Sutton
> Aircraft Commander
> 45th Bombardment Group (H)
> Bassingbourn, England

CHAPTER ONE

The shattered B-17 began to die before it reached the English Channel, slipping now like a great limp bird through the last 2,800 feet. In the distance, through the cracked and webbed Plexiglass, through the sea mist and smoke-haze, the pilot—Capt. James L. Sutton—could barely see the majestic upsweep of the craggy coastline. After four missions the bomber was a pained and bleeding creature falling from the sky for the last time.

In front of the copilot's station, the quarter-panel windscreen had been blown inward fifteen minutes ago over Metz, France. The copilot dangled limp in his harness; the blood-soaked form bounced with each vibration of the disintegrating ship.

The Bendix chin-turret had exploded a few seconds later, when the two Focke-Wulf Fw-190s made their last blistering head-on sweep. They were dash 3 models from

Jagdgeschwader Richthofen 2 based in France. The commander, Maj. Hellmuth Hund, and his adjutant, the aristocratic *Hauptman* Prince Ritter von Woll, came skidding in from the sun's pale disc. Their 1,700-horsepower BMW radial engines roared in harmony as the 20mm *Oerlikon* machine guns fragmented the nose canopy into a cloud of glassy snow. For an instant, within a range of twenty yards, Major Hund saw the oxygen-masked face of the bombardier looking up, surprised. His hands were frozen on the handles of the .50-caliber guns. The major saw the white-hot paths of the tracers jetting past; the last thing the bombardier saw was the quick glint of silver bullion on the collar patches of the major's leather flight jacket. Two-tenths of a second after the canopy fragmented, three high-explosive cannon shells ignited the ammunition links in the chin-turret. The batch of ammo exploded, ripped apart sheet metal, and tore the guns loose. The explosion blew a jagged hole in front of the starboard cheekgun. The bombardier thought someone had sliced his face open with a knife; he was heaved through the opening. As he fell, his parachute pack aflame, he wondered what time it was; he vomited, falling end over end through nine thousand damp, hazy feet of French air. He hit a dirt road and left an indentation three feet deep and three feet wide. The navigator, a 21-year old second lieutenant, had been sitting behind the bombardier when he heard the blast. He was sliced in half by the shock force and flying fragments from the Norden bombsight. The upper half of his torso sailed down above the bombardier; an atomized plume of red fluid marked his descent.

The destruction had begun over Metz twenty minutes ago, after the bomb run, when a quartet of 88mm shells caught the B-17—*The Lazy Lady*—but did not destroy her outright. She continued to stumble along, losing altitude, a weak bird about to be pounced by Hund and his adjutant; they were scrambling then in an attempt to attack stragglers.

The four 88's were direct hits and made contact with *The Lazy Lady* within a time frame of seven seconds. The first of the kill-cluster exploded within the open but empty bomb bay, instantly killing the radio operator and severely wounding the belly gunner. The second and third hits exploded simultaneously and destroyed both inboard engines. The fourth tore through the vertical stabilizer and, because of a faulty detonator, failed to explode. Most of the bomber's controls were inoperative; the trimming handle and wheel, which control the angle of the ship for landing, were destroyed; the throttles were partially jammed in the mangled throttle-quadrant, and the interphone and radio were inoperable.

"We're not going to make it!" Sutton screamed over the gale force, not knowing that the copilot had been dead for four minutes.

Captain Sutton was from New York but he loved England. He wanted her desperately. In the distance he could see the tall bluffs from Eastbourn to Bexhill-on-the-Sea, where the wonderful scent of salt water rode thick drafts of damp English air—that stretch of coast where plump sea gulls danced nervously with the English breeze that swept inward over fields of golden harvest. He wished he were a gull, safe out there, doing lazy circles with the wind, defying gravity.

Oh how he wanted to live! To make a pact with the devil if it would mean keeping alive. He wanted to make it! To come alive again. To be reborn! He wanted to see those wonderful historic towns and cities down there: Guildford, Horsham, Dorking, the train station in London. He wanted his warm sack and his familiar pillow. He could sleep for five days and nights and then have glasses of beer and steak and onions and hot apple pie and a warm brandy and a good cigar.

He was so tired!

She came into focus again, Allison with the green eyes. She always did in moments of desperation, and he wanted to hear her tell him, *Yes I do love you and I do care so very much and please come back home for me.*

But he knew if she did, if she said that, it would be a lie, that he would be lying to himself. She stood there and said nothing and stared at his hands, frozen like her eyes on the spidery Plexiglass, her silky brown hair unruffled by the beating jet wind. She was cold, not from the driving wind, but from within herself, and that's what he hated about her. Couldn't she see him suffering out here, halfway to death for Christ's sake! Why couldn't she write? How could she not find the time, five minutes, to sit down and jot out a note, to show concern? Anything would've been fine. The weather. Gossip. He saw her outstretched in front of the fireplace, eyes half-open, a faint smile on thin determined lips. Her nipples were the color of the flames. Above the thick odor of burnt flesh and gunsmoke and oil and gasoline, he could taste her; and he knew that she didn't give a one simple toot if he lived or smashed into the Channel. That's how much she cared.

God! Couldn't he try again and get it right the second time? Another chance. Just one more!

"Captain! Captain!"

If he could just see her one more time; convince her how much he loved her, how much he really cared.

"Captain! Can you hear me!" a voice yelled, implored over the 100-mile-an-hour gale slicing through the windscreen. The voice — and he was not quite certain of this — could not be Allison's; she was far away, snug as a bug in her father's twelve-room house. (What time was it on the East Coast? He could never remember the damned difference between here and there and wondered if *that* meant anything; if it meant that he really didn't care or love his lovely iceberg lady after all). No, the voice hadn't her soft, whispery tone; didn't have the accents in the right places. Besides, she never raised her voice above anything. Hers was the voice of a lazy lady. The voice he heard was the voice of a desperate man. That he was certain of. Was he dreaming or dying? Maybe he was on the verge of death. Maybe this was what it was like; he didn't know. Everything was hazy. Milky. Or had the glass splinters in his bleeding forehead penetrated his brain? He remembered someone telling him that bright red blood was okay — that it merely came from capillaries near the skin's surface — but if you saw blood the color of rich dark wine, that was serious stuff, and if it kept pouring out you'd go into shock, and your lights would be out in a matter of minutes. Then you wouldn't have to worry about women who never wrote. But this voice, deep and familiar, was real. It came through his lightheadedness with thick screaming stabs.

"Captain Sutton! It's me!"

Sutton looked at the copilot. It couldn't

be him; half his head was gone. If he didn't pull the limp form up soon it would tumble over the control column; and he knew that he didn't have the strength left to pull him away. A dead man would kill him and take Allison down with them and they would finally rest together in a strange channel of water between France and England. What shitty luck!

"Captain Sutton it's me! Tutone!"

Sutton turned quickly, fearing to take his eyes off the instruments, what was left of them, off the horizon of England that kept *The Lazy Lady's* wings level. It was a physical and psychological effort to turn his head.

A gloved hand, tattered, stretched out for him and grabbed his shoulder. When Sutton's eyes focused he saw Benny Tutone. The glove was smeared with blood.

"I can't help you!"

"The blood's not mine, sir," Tutone said. "It's Wilson's. I tried, but he fell through a hole in the radio compartment. He's gone. Into the sea. No parachute. Couldn't hold him."

The ship's nose pitched down and the horizon, which Sutton had neglected, had risen toward the sky. They were diving for the Channel, drawn there by the weight of the dead copilot draped over the control column. His arms flapped as if to disavow any responsibility for the body's deadly action:

13

I'm really sorry about this, Jim, but, you see, I have no control over life anymore because I've just lost my head and please forgive. . . .

"Get him off!" Sutton screamed. "He's dead! I can't pull up."

If they had stood a chance of making their base, now they would barely reach within miles of the place. Fuel was spilling through the fuel tanks. Soon the engines would sputter and then there would be silence and gravity would tell them where they were going to land, where they would crash and die.

What really shitty luck. A dead man was driving them into the Channel!

Sutton reached out for the copilot's collar. Tutone released the seatbelt harness. He mumbled something when he came near the shattered head, then they both pulled back and struggled with the dead weight.

"Get him out of here," Sutton commanded.

At a thousand feet he regained control and had *The Lazy Lady* straight and level again. England was coming closer.

Bassingbourn, his airbase. . . . Sutton tried to recall the countryside, tried to remember bicycle rides and walks down shaded lanes, car trips on the wrong side of the road. If he could recall the land it would offer a chance. He needed a safe place to crash-land his airplane because he knew he wouldn't make Bassingbourn. He calculated altitude, rate of descent, distance, fuel remaining, power left in the coughing engines. He was certain now that Bassingbourn was too far off to reach.

The Lazy Lady was quivering, certain of her own death. She was dropping like a dinner plate.

Sutton remembered Bassett, the muscular pilot from Vermont who played Cole Porter on the piano in the Officers' Club—he was lying crushed in the cockpit of *Bombs Away*. That was the day he fell short of the north-south runway and hit a low, ancient stone wall built by some Knight of the Roundtable a thousand years ago. How could he have known? Unless he knew the land, unless he knew what a damned stone wall four feet high could do to a speeding bomber skidding along a cow pasture. Too much Cole Porter and beer and not enough knowledge of the land.

The Lazy Lady passed over the coast; she couldn't be steered effectively. She was telling Sutton where *she* wanted to go.

Four hundred, maybe five hundred feet, slipping down, roaring over no-name towns and villages. It was too late to bail out. He should've thought of that sooner. He failed his crew.

He loved them all. Oh Lord how he loved them! How close he felt to them, to their spirits, fused by the fuselage of their great ship. A machine of destruction had drawn

15

them together in the sky, had given them a singular life, a sole purpose. He had written to Allison about them:

Here in the sky we are one. Only on Earth are we separate. We all move the same way and at the same time up there. We breathe the same, feel the same pain, the same joy. We care about each other, for each of us is no different than the other.

Poetic, he thought at the time. But true. Because without saying so, they had drawn together. Men under attack, each fearful of losing his life but willing to help and protect his comrades. A forceful rule of nature, as long as time had brought them close than they would be to anyone else for the rest of their lives. Young men with shiny faces and flat bellies, some without beards to shave and eyes that still had the sparkle of hope, the promise of tomorrow. The joy that comes with living! He loved them all, and now they were all gone. Seretsky, the esthetic tail gunner; Ruppert, who would've been a priest; Wilson, the radioman who seldom smiled; Baylor and Scoon, the waistgunners who were dating sisters; Torres, the belly gunner, frozen to death; and young Freeman, the bombardier who couldn't shoot straight. And Benson, the copilot, who kept saying he would never get home alive. *You were right, Benson, absolutely right.*

"Can you do it, boss?" asked Tutone.

"I never crashed a B-17 before."

He had only force-landed a plane once—
a single-engine, paint-peeling, oil-smeared
Travel Air 4000 K with a busted fuel gauge
and control lines lousy with too much play.
A real heap. Billy Hayes dared him to go up
in the thing. Hayes said, "You don't have
the balls to fly it." Sutton took it up. A
couple of spins, loops and sloppy snap rolls
around the field and Sutton realized he had
a fuel gauge that was stuck. After the prop
stopped he aimed for a field and came down
silently. The wind harped across the scratchy
paint, and below he saw Hayes rolling on the
sparkling grass. He was holding his sides,
laughing, pointing his finger at the sky. Son-
of-a-bitch! Sutton brought the plane across
the cow pasture then dropped it. Before he
stopped rolling the tail came over his head,
the wheels having struck solid rock and dirt.
He hung in the cockpit upside down,
laughing, tears dripping from his eyes, glad
to be alive. He didn't unhook his harness
because someone had told him that as soon
as you do that you drop and snap your neck.
Hayes, laughing, unhooked him and then
Sutton punched him in the nose.

But he never crash-landed a bomber
before. He never had to worry about a plane
exploding, or ammunition cooking off while
he tried to escape twisted metal.

*Well, this is the way it's going to be and
you'd better resign yourself,* he thought.
Going to take a pigged out B-17, a disinter-

grating wreck and a dead crew, and put it down.

He never imagined it would end this way. He had always felt there was something heroic in store. Not this!

There was something gallant about going off to fight this war, something about his youth that protected him from the true vision of battle and death. Even now it was hard to comprehend.

He looked down briefly and saw the golden harvest, the potato fields and pastures, the villages, the dirt roads and streams, and the sparkling grass. Billy Hayes wasn't there; he was home safe, 4-F, probably still laughing. The son-of-a-bitch!

Tutone leaned into Sutton's ear: "Where are you going to put it, boss?"

"Into a fuckin' stone wall!"

Tutone half-believed him.

The Lazy Lady could no longer be steered. It slipped past a town with no familiar form or shape, with no relationship to Bassingbourn. To hell with the map—he didn't have time, no time left at all.

The frayed and strained cables were finally coming apart. What remained was jammed in the twisted, blackened metal along the ship's body. Pieces of tail section and burning chunks of engine parts had fallen off and marked the ship's sinking flight path.

Now, there was a loud rip—the bomb bay

doors peeled off and fell away. Souvenirs of a dead ship. Two large potato fields loomed ahead, broken by a slim dirt road with low hedgerows. The road would be long enough but the wingspan—104 feet—would overlap the road's edges. It would be a feat merely to slap the bomber down on the road, Sutton thought. He would have to cut power at precisely the right moment and drop the ship like a boulder.

He was hunched over the control column, a rigid, sweating figure, toying with mushy ailerons and the remains of the elevators. He felt for the ganged throttles and quickly glanced at the oil-smeared starboard engine. The smoke-stained nacelle stuttered, then the prop jerked to a halt. The remaining engine backfired and choked, ready to die. The engine racket scattered geese and cows. A final cough and the prop windmilled lazily in the rush of the slipstream. Sutton could see a dog looking up in the distance, on the road, amazed and bewildered at the sight of the bomber speeding toward him. The dog was frozen, slack-jawed. He had seen plenty of bombers skipping over the fields and trees and through the clouds, and he was aware of the sound they made.

"Get the hell out of there, you dumb bastard!"

The dog sprinted for a field and looked back just once. The great smoking thing was still falling from the sky. It created a mad, billowing black cloud that pointed to the spot he'd run from.

Sutton kicked hard left rudder. He lined *The Lady* up with the middle of the road. He jerked the control column back, deep into his lap, and felt the ship falter and hesitate. It came over the center of the road and stalled. It felt sweet, a heavenly motion, he thought, momentarily proud of his action, his ability. He began counting the distance before the ship impacted—forty, thirty, twenty. . . .

Ten feet.

For a few seconds everything was peaceful, quiet.

The Lazy Lady floated like a battered woman in a swimming pool before thudding onto the cement bottom. She was fully ballooned. If the wheels were down this would've been a perfect landing. A peach. There was one final quiver, a loud bang. Something in the back ripped off and flew away. The jagged remains of the ball turret hit the road first.

Sutton, still intoxicated with his landing approach, pushed the wheel forward and tried to maintain the perfect landing. But there was nothing left in the controls. His motion was pilot reflex. When the tail hit, the nose jerked up with a thunderous roar and then the tail banged down with sledge-hammer force. The shock blinded him for an instant. The plane hit the road with a crackling, deafening sound. The hedges slipped past. The wingtips fluttered. The props curled and cut swaths along the road's edges.

Fire!

That's what he feared most as he sat there helpless.

The whole thing's going to go up in flames!

The Lady slid sideways and headed for a deep drainage ditch. Sutton pressed his quick-release harness button and listened for the primary pop of exploding fuel cells. The nose buried into the side of the ditch, and then the metal scream ended. The ship stopped.

There was silence. A wren flew past the shattered windscreen. A flock of sparrows settled into a tree.

Sutton heard himself breathing, and through the sawing sound he remembered Tutone. He yelled over his shoulder, trying to unscramble his limbs from the mesh of wire and metal. "Tutone! Do you hear me! Where are you?" Then his body stopped moving.

He seemed frozen in his seat—as if he weren't allowed to abandon *The Lady* in her moment of final disgrace.

God, he could never recall being this tired. The war had lost its rhyme, its reason. Something in his mind snapped. Not before Metz, not when the shells exploded, not when he realized he might die—but now, when he felt sure he would live.

He felt distant, detached from himself—from everything.

"Boss! Are you okay?" Tutone pulled Sutton's legs clear of the twisted instrument panel, pulling him towards a hole in the fuselage. Both of them were desperate now, fearful of an explosion.

In the clear light, a young Girl Scout with rosy cheeks appeared under Sutton's window. She peered into the wrecked cockpit. Her face radiated horror; she was speechless. She saw Benson's head and gagged.

"Get away!" Sutton yelled at her. "Run!" The girl's face vanished and she began running toward the field's edge.

Sutton and Tutone followed her. Don't think about it, Sutton thought. Just keep running and don't look back. His legs pounded over the springy earth, his flying boots kicking at those glorious English stones. He was on the ground. And now he wanted more. He wanted to live, to leave the wreck, this field. With each gasping stride through the sweet English air, his lungs burned and his arms pumped with a fury he had never known. He felt like a child again. A ghost, some night spirit, was coming after him, running behind him in the deep dark of the nightmare. Don't stop. Run!

Tutone was fast. Faster than both of them. They said he was built like that popular singer, Frank Sinatra: slim, wiry. The wind caught his thick black pompadour. Run!

Think about something else, Sutton said to himself. Concentrate. Focus on the stone wall. Keep pumping. Find more strength. Please! Find more. Don't miss a beat. His arms got heavy and his long wavy brown hair stung his eyes. Run!

Tutone reached the wall and jumped over and tumbled down, exhausted. The girl came over next. Sutton slowed just before he reached them; he crawled over the top. His body filled with pain; he could barely see; sweat burned his eyes. After a few seconds, Sutton and Tutone lifted themselves. Their arms were around each other's shoulders and they stared at their dead ship. She was crumpled—a dead, beaten animal. Smoke rose from her engines.

Tutone said. "Ain't gonna blow, boss."

There was a brilliant flash of light and one second later *The Lazy Lady* exploded, disappearing in an orange ball of fire and smoke. Thunder echoed across the still fields, diffused, then met itself again.

There was little left of her—a few shreds of metal, the tail assembly, the twisted wingtips pointing to the sky. Birds dissipated and flew off in nervous patterns. The girl silently reached out for Sutton's hand and grasped it strongly.

Sirens cried in the distance.

CHAPTER TWO

Two young gunners, Bush and Skolinsky, were standing on the lawn outside Bassingbourn's medical building killing time, watching the Fortresses sweep around the clear sky, surveying the air field like two cocky rich kids in the market for prime property. Within minutes they had discussed the prospects for obtaining dames, their barracks, the quality of the chow, the hangars, and the reasons they felt they had been assigned to a new aircraft.

"We were doing all right in the old plane," Bush said. "What the hell did they change us for?" He got a grunt of agreement from Skolinsky.

They had been on English soil less than three weeks but proved themselves. Each had two kills to his credit and everyone was impressed. Already the war had given them a tingle, a feeling they had never dreamed possible; they felt electrified. The reality of war and its machinery had finally begun to

24

swell before their twinkling eyes. The air had a unique odor. The roar of Wright Turbo super-charged engines, the scent of aviation fuel, was like the incense of battle floating before the altar of youth. They were young and eager and yearned for combat. They were willing to die, not believing they would; they were brash, yet humble; they were hopeful, but not idealistic; they were casual, but not arrogant; they were young, but not virginal. Two young gunners standing on the lawn outside Bassingbourn's medical building, waiting to see their new aircraft commander.

A military police jeep popped through the heat haze. Its siren wailed as it came toward them.

Bush took out a pack of Camels and offered one to Skolinsky. "Shit," Bush said, watching the jeep, "I hope he's better than old Bremmer."

The siren grew fuller and the jeep turned toward them.

Bush asked, "What's the pilot's name?"

"Sutton. James Sutton."

They had come here ten minutes ago to satisfy their curiosity. They wanted to see their new command pilot.

The jeep slipped to a halt twenty yards away. Two MPs jumped out. Sutton was staring through the windshield. The MPs reached for him, but Sutton threw his hand up and refused their assistance.

"That's him," said Skolinsky, bringing his cigarette up to his mouth. He studied the figure moving from the jeep.

The MPs escorted Sutton into the medical building.

Bush shrugged his shoulders. "Okay. We saw him, now let's get something to eat."

Inside the medical building Doctor Matlin got up and stepped across to the cabinets and took out a file and kicked the drawer closed and came back, lighting up a smoke.

"No one thought you'd be coming back," he said.

"Why not?" Sutton asked.

"You were overdue. A few of the crews reported that they saw you get hit and that there wasn't a chance you'd—"

"Sorry to disappoint everybody."

Matlin gave an unbalanced grin. "It must've been rough," he said.

"Oh come on for shit's sake and let me go," Sutton shot back. "I've got a scratch on my head. I need a little sleep and I'll be okay."

Matlin opened the file and took his sweet time, pressing his finger under *Sutton, James L.*, because he'd seen them before like this when they'd just come back after smashing one up badly, walking away from it as if they didn't give a hoot about it. Of course that wasn't true, and it always took time for them to cool off, to come down before weeping like a child who'd lost something they'd never get back again. They were all the same. All of them except Sutton.

In the distance some mechanic wasn't satisfied with an engine and had tweaked it up till it seemed it would burst. The sound vibrated the walls, filled the office with a drone.

"All right," Matlin said, and squinted through a cloud of cigarette smoke. "How do you feel?"

"I'll feel a lot better when I leave this building. Can't we get on with this for God's sakes?"

Matlin looked down at the file again and spread his stubby white fingers like big fans. Slowly, he said, "You must feel something after losing eight men and crash-landing a Fort."

"I feel sorry, all right? Does that make you happy? Other than that, there's really nothing to discuss."

Matlin eyed the medical file again, Sutton's vital stats, medical history, and so on.

The mechanic apparently took pleasure in revving engines because he had this one screaming at the top of the RPM arc and it sounded ready to pop. If he let it go anymore at that level it would heat. The air filled with its shrill tone, wavering, spilling off the walls, coming through the cracks of the place.

"Son-of-a-bitch is going to bust the jugs," said Sutton.

Matlin would've agreed but he didn't know anything about engines and cylinder head temperatures. Right now he was concerned with a pilot that wouldn't talk. He poured two Scotches and slid one across the veneer. "This'll take the edge off," he said.

There was a knock at the door.

A sergeant came quietly to the desk and placed another file on the blotter. It was Sutton's 66-1, his personnel file and it said more than the boring medical charts Matlin pushed aside. It said that Sutton was the number one pilot in his former squadron, that he was insubordinate and brash, respected by his men, and on the verge of a court-martial.

Matlin, without looking up, asked. "What'd you do before the war?"

"I was a crop duster and helped my father run a small airfield," Sutton said, downing the Scotch.

"It says here that your license was suspended for thirty days."

Sutton smiled. "I flew under some high-voltage wires and a bridge, that's all. Nobody got hurt and I had a hell of a time. The only thing was, some old bastard copied my numbers and reported me."

"What happened over Metz?" asked Matlin, pouring another shot.

"It was simple. All standard procedure.

We took an hour to form up, had P-47 escort. It started out a milk run, very little flak. Over the target, we salvoed our bombs and turned home. After we straightened out there were four quick kicks." He paused for a few seconds then said, "We took four direct hits. Bam! Bam! Bam! Bam!" He slapped his fist on the desk top.

"Would believe that?" He held up four fingers and shook them for emphasis, then he continued: "The interphone went out and I had very little idea what occurred. Tutone said that he saw Seretsky, the tail gunner, bail out before we reached the Channel. Because of fuel tank damage, we ran out before Bassingbourn." He took more Scotch, and after a few second's silence he said, "I'll never forget it, that's for damned sure."

Matlin offered a smoke and Sutton took one and rolled the wheel of a Zippo his father had given him before he left for England. The Zippo had been with his father for years, a gift from his mother months before she died. She had one word engraved on it: *Gimper*. A gimper was a superior aviator, someone who'd fly through anything, land on a napkin, rip apart an engine blindfolded, or get good and drunk and fly zipper-up through a cockeyed tunnel. A gimper was more than an ace aviator. A gimper had ability but didn't boast about it; he took flying seriously, but not himself. A gimper was a guy you'd want up front when one engine on a single-engine plane busted out during a blizzard. Like his father, Sutton was a gimper. To anyone else the lighter was a lighter, but when Sutton rolled the spark wheel he had his father in his palm. The lighter had sat lost on a Mexican runway paved with flattened mosquitos and lizards for three months; it lit the cigarettes and cigars of hucksters, con men, and jerks from Florida to Maine. It had been rained on, snowed on, stepped on, used as a screwdriver and as a hammer. It was valuable; it had raw gut meaning. If someone opened it they'd see Sutton inside. A dog pissed on it once out of arrogance at a Pennsylvania airfield. One night over Cape May, New Jersey, it lit the instruments on Sutton's plane when the lights fizzed out. It was a rabbit's foot. When old man Sutton handed it to Jim he didn't have to think twice about it — it wasn't a father handing a wad of bills or a money-making business to a grateful son; it was a craggy-faced gimper giving his son a fistful of memories, and there weren't any damned bands playing or speeches made. When he squeezed it into Jim's palm, he said, "Your asshole's a little punchy, so you're going to need this more than me." And that was all. That's how they left each other at the train station.

Sutton took in smoke and knew that what he had to get off his mind was going to disappoint everyone: Allison, who probably wouldn't give a pill anyway; his father; his buddy Hayes; his new commanding officer, Col. Branch Parker; and everyone else who knew Sutton and expected more. They would be surprised. He didn't want to say what he had on his mind, but the words came spilling out.

"I'm supposed to report to Colonel Parker this afternoon but I don't want to because I don't want to fly under his command."

The doctor grunted. He let out some air—like a spectator watching a third baseman making a poor play for the ball. He thought of himself now, his task as a doctor, as a man who had to keep these pilots flying. *They have really given me too much,* Matlin thought. *I've kept my part and came here from a wall-busting practice in Seattle; but they have asked me to perform miracles.* They wanted a medical doctor, a pill-pusher, an administrator, and a psychiatrist for wayward, broken airmen. It was a pain in the ass, he felt, and there wasn't a pill for it. Every time one of these boys stood up and wept about no more flying, it was on Matlin to get that boy's butt hung on straight so he could be back in the air. They needed everyone they had, he was told by Colonel Parker, and everyone they had was needed. No exceptions. That was the Army Air Force way. Nice and simple.

"I don't understand," Matlin said, looking puzzled. "why you can't fly for Branch

31

Parker. It was my understanding that today's mission over Metz was your last mission with your old Group, and that you were to transfer to Parker's Group for a very special reason." His voice underlined *very special* with a mysterious tone.

"True. But that doesn't mean I have to like it. Or, for that matter, that I will fly for him."

"I mean," said Matlin, "I can't see it. I can't figure you of all people for not wanting to fly. You've got fourteen missions under your belt. You're not a novice. You—"

"I didn't say I didn't want to fly. First of all, I'll be honest with you, Doc," Sutton said, brushing back his deep brown hair. "I ain't too anxious about going back up and getting my ass shot at again. But that's not it. I just don't want to fly for Parker. I was volunteered for this transfer."

"But it's apparently a special mission."

"I don't give a shit if it's flying for Santa Claus."

Matlin shook his head. He took another swallow of Scotch. Licking his lips slowly, he said. "Our commanding officer here, Colonel Parker, really wants to keep the Group and the component squadrons up to full strength. He's not going to like it if you go in and tell him you don't want to fly."

"You're not listening to me, Doc. I said I'd fly okay, but it's just that I don't think I want to fly for Parker."

Parker wanted his boys up in the air, not on the ground. Feeble excuses, medical nonsense, and psychiatric mumbo-jumbo no longer cut the mustard. Matlin's neck was on the block if some pilot had decided enough was enough. "My boys," Parker had said with a thick Midwestern drawl, "fly. They do not walk, they do not talk, and they do not swim. They all fly. Make myself clear, Matlin?"

Matlin looked down at the folder then said, "These pages are filled with complimentary remarks about you. You were a pilot prior to your service—"

"I was a bush-banging crop-duster, is all."

Matlin ran a finger across the typed sentence. "You were rated number one in your training class."

"True. The next three are dead. Wayne Edmund busted apart over France and there were no chutes from his bird. Ed Hearle died here after crash-landing at the end of the runway. And Fred Schwartz had his leg blown off and then bled to death. Look," Sutton said, leaning toward the desk, "there's no doubt I'm the best pilot around, but that doesn't mean I have to love flying for Parker."

"I can't accept that." Matlin let out some air.

"You don't have to." Sutton bit the inside of his mouth.

The mechanic was playing a different

tune now, goosing up the engine in huge waves of sound. "He's going to wreck that fucker," Sutton said.

"I don't know anything about engines, Captain. I'm having a hard enough time understanding pilots."

Sutton looked at Matlin. The rose light turned the window panes fiery red and bathed the doctor's frail face a tarnished gold. Sutton felt sorry for the doctor. Maybe it was because Parker had influenced his life, his ability to judge others.

Matlin said, "Colonel Parker is having a press conference outside his office in a little while—he's introducing a new copilot. He asked me to tell you to meet him there."

Sutton shrugged his shoulders. "Well, Doc, thanks for the tea and sympathy." He stood and walked to the door and twisted the knob and turned and looked at the small figure with the golden face and said:

"Parker's a nasty son-of-a-bitch, and you know it. They don't call him Irontail for nothing. He's egotistical and self-centered and ambitious, and you know that, too. He drives his men for his own needs and really has little concern for them. And if that isn't sufficient reason not to fly for the bastard, I don't know what is."

"That's a challenging statement, Captain."

"Well, here's another one for you: How would *you* like to fly for Parker?"

CHAPTER THREE

Sutton stood with a group of sixteen reporters a short distance from Colonel Parker's office. They were chatting, trading favorite anecdotes, waiting impatiently for the Colonel to appear. They were from the major news services: *The New York Times, Colliers, Stars & Stripes, The Saturday Evening Post,* Hearst, Black Starr, Associated Press, NBC, and Mutual Radio. Allen Bender of the New York *Daily Mirror,* said that he heard that Rag Tag, Colonel Parker's German shepherd, had gotten laid earlier that morning. "It was some horny English sheep dog who just *adores* American airmen. Now he's worried that he might have gotten her pregnant."

Symns, from *The London Times,* begged for a hasty introduction to the English bitch; this brought a ripple of soft laughter.

Rag Tag looked up, blinked his long heavy lashes, then set his forlorn jowls down across his meaty paws.

"Shit!" *Colliers'* Jones said. "You pissed him off!"

More laughter, words of agreement.

Patterson from AP walked over to Rag Tag, but before he reached him the dog stood and went slowly toward Parker's jeep a few feet away. He raised a leg and took a leak on the front tire.

"Oh Jesus!" shouted Patterson. "Call the Colonel! Someone's destroying government property."

Rag Tag looked up, sleepy-eyed, bewildered.

Sutton lit a cigarette and looked into the sky.

An English Supermarine *Spitfire* Mk. II was circling the base; this was its second sweep, the brown-eyed flyer observed. The ship was in slow flight, barely above stall speed. It was two hundred feet above the ground; the spinach and brown camouflage and English roundels on the fuselage were crisp in the clear light. When it turned, it went gradually, the wings hardly tipping.

Jones looked at his watch; he was annoyed. He could've been flying in a P-38 *Lightning* today, one of the Air Force's hot new pursuit ships; but instead of sweeping over France shooting up rail lines, he took Parker's invitation to meet a *dynamic new member of the 45th Bombardment Group.* He kicked a rock and sent it lofting toward the snoozing Rag Tag. "I'm getting too old for this shit," Jones said. He looked at his watch again and noted that Parker and the "dynamic new member" were ten minutes late.

"Typical," Sutton told him.

Symns and Patterson agreed. They were salty veterans of the press with unmatched credentials, fresh from air and naval action in the Pacific Theatre. They'd been shot down, shot at, wounded, and insulted; they had covered MacArthur and Stilwell, spent time in the Pentagon and training camps, eaten with G.I.'s from Tripoli to Anzio, and seen ships and men go down at Pearl Harbor. And now they'd been put on hold by a chicken colonel who promised to give them something dynamic.

A fuel truck chugged past them and headed for the flight-line. Two mechanics in greasy coveralls stood in the distance studying the group. Three nurses from the base hospital walked up to the reporters and asked what they were waiting for. Jones answered quickly, "We're waiting for something *dynamic* to happen." The nurses smiled, three lovely cookies impressed by the large gathering of media.

The *Spitfire* made another low sweep, wings level, the engine thrumming in the low RPM range.

At 0816, Colonel Parker stepped from his office, dressed in freshly pressed Class A's. His driver, Sergeant Cole, trailed behind.

Rag Tag stood and met his master. When Parker hit the center of the group, another figure exited from the doorway—a tall, blond-haired, blue-eyed bomber pilot with first lieutenant's bars glistening in the sharp sunlight; he wore a hand-tailored uniform from Brooks Brothers. The crowd began to mumble as they formed a horseshoe around Parker.

Jones whispered to Symns, "Does that look dynamic to you?"

Flash bulbs popped, wire recorders began, pencils started scratching. Parker was beaming. The crowd had grown now; more nurses, mechanics, a few of the cooks from the nearby Officers' Mess, some people from Intelligence, Weather, a couple of Red Cross ladies.

Parker finally dropped the bomb. "Gentlemen," he said, "thank you for your patience. I've asked you here for a special reason. As you know, the 45th Bombardment Group is composed of America's finest young men. And so, it is with pleasure that I announce a new addition to our already outstanding roster of excellent airmen— airmen who bring with them the courage, experience, and desire necessary to defeat the Nazi threat." He turned and held out his arm and drew in the first lieutenant. "Gentlemen, meet Lieutenant Roger Griffin."

"Shit," Sutton said quietly.

Symns turned to Sutton. "What'd you say?"

"Do you know who that is?"

Symns shook his head.

"Roger, the boy aviator," Sutton said. "The world's most outstanding three-dollar phony."

Symns appeared perplexed.

In a whispered tone, Sutton said: "Did you ever hear of the *outside loop?*"

"Sure. A few years ago some kid —" He turned and looked into the lieutenant's boyish face.

"You're lookin' at it in the flesh, old boy," Sutton said.

Griffin came from husky New York money. Very large bucks; big family influence. The family was the Griffin Aircraft Corporation, known simply through the world of aviation as GAC. The addresses were Palm Beach, Palm Springs, and Poughkeepsie, New York, not far from the town where Sutton grew up. The Griffin image was two-pronged: the one the world knew and the one Sutton knew. Neither were close to each other. The Griffin influence was worldwide. Roger as a child knew senators, playboys, princes and kings, pretenders of the first rank, monied people, and people who looked monied. A Yale graduate, Roger had been knighted with a GAC vice presidency at nineteen. He'd been flying since he was thirteen. What drew

Roger toward flying was the glamour. Glamour was sex.

At nineteen, Roger copped second place in the world-famous Thompson Trophy Air Race, only, some said, because Roger's father paid off the other aviators in the race. The world began to notice the "boy aviator," as he was becoming known.

On the 15th of April, 1938, GAC announced that Roger would attempt to fly the dreaded outside loop—which required the mentality of a maniac mixed with the gall of a flea contemplating intercourse with an elephant.

Until then, because of aircraft limitations, the outside loop had been achieved by only a handful of fearless aviators. No one Roger's age, however, had attempted its suicide path—at least no one known to the world. Inside loops, though, were common—the pilot flew straight and level into the bottom of a large imaginary ferris wheel, pulled back on the control column and went nose up, scribing a circle around the inside of the wheel, flying out level again from the point where he began. In this maneuver, pilot and plane are upside down at the top of the wheel. The outside loop is just the opposite—the pilot flies toward the top of the wheel, pushes *forward* on the control column and goes nose down, scribing a circle around the *outside* of the wheel, and flies out level again from the point of entry.

Here, pilot and plane are upside down at the bottom of the arc.

On the 8th of May, 1938, Roger suited up and strapped on a Griffin custom-built RG-4 *Aerohound*. It was so low, so sleek, that it looked like a cross between a whippet and a snake. Someone said that if you didn't watch yourself you'd walk on it. When Roger uncorked the jewel-like four-cyinder engine, the crowd went drunk with excitement. They cooed like a baby smelling warm chocolate. Melanie Thomas, Roger's number one cookie, nearly dropped her silk Saks Fifth Avenue panties right there on the hot tarmac. To her, blue exhaust smoke was more intoxicating than amber perfume.

Ernst Udet, the outstanding World War I German flying ace, whom Herman Goering would anoint as head of the *Luftwaffe's* Technical Department, was one of the babes in the crowd. Anyone who was anyone in aviation circles was there, delighted, waiting for Roger to bust a spar on the apex of the loop and come down in several pieces before going splat on the ground.

Roger had let the oil thin while the press snapped picture after picture. "Build up some tension, kid," the senior Griffin told Roger. "Don't just fire it up and take off. Make 'em think you're exploring your soul and mind before you lift the old *hound off the ground.*"

Three days before, two men in gray

double-breasted suits drove down from Poughkeepsie in a maroon Chevvy and offered Jim Sutton ten thousand dollars. "What for?" Sutton asked them. "We've got a new airplane that's never been flown before, and we want you to try an outside loop in it. If you agree, you have to sign a waiver and a sworn statement that you won't tell anyone that the plane belongs to Griffin Aviation." Sutton needed the dough, so he signed up. The next day he did two outside loops, thanked the men and signed the papers, paid off his father's mortgage, and forgot the matter.

The Griffins were then certain Roger's *Aerohound* could handle the trick; they were also sure Roger would do it. Udet was amazed. He kept snapping his kid gloves in his palm, shaking his head, saying, "Dis is remarkable. Dis is truly remarkable." Udet knew. He had seen a British pilot in World War I try an outside loop while being pursued. The ship came apart like a Kleenex box in a typhoon.

The *Aerohound* zipped into the sky. *Roger performed a few aerial hors d'oeuvres first: Cuban Eights, Immelmans, power-on, power-off stalls, a very crisp clover leaf, just to warm up the wings before he attempted to enter aerobatic heaven.*

Then the PA system made the announcement: "Ladies and gentemen. . . . Mister Roger Griffin will now attempt the difficult and deadly outside loop."

As Roger entered the loop the crowd screamed, men cursed, children's jaws went slack and their eyes lit up like emergency light bulbs.

Roger missed. Something went wrong.

He snapped the hound over on her right wing and broke away from the scribed approach and entered a very screwy barrel roll.

The crowd was sweating.

What they didn't know was that Roger had planned this, that all this was mere aerial bullshit. He had them in the palm of his hand.

On the second sweep Roger hit the razzle-dazzle button. The crowd roared like a pleased beast. Melanie thought this would surely make this evening's orgasm that much sweeter.

Roger hit the loop flawlessly. The *Aerohound* slipped through the turn like a duck paddling round a water lily. Exquisite. Women nearly fainted. Children roared with glee. Men applauded. The press ran for phones. R.G.'s son did it.

The Griffin Aircraft Company received excellent press. Roger's boyish peach-toned face was all over the planet:

*R.G. GRIFFIN FLIES OUTSIDE
LOOP*
POUGHKEEPSIE, N.Y., May
8—*Roger G. Griffin, 18, was the second*

man in three years to fly the dreaded "outside loop." Mr. Griffin, the son of R. Turner Griffin, president of the Griffin Aircraft Company, Poughkeepsie, New York, is the youngest man to fly the outside loop. A crowd of nearly a thousand, including the World War I German flying ace, Ernst Udet, witnessed the feat.

Roger and the *Aerohound* went on national tour. Melanie remained behind. "Oh . . . faster . . . please . . . faster," she whispered on the evening of Roger's spectacular event, knowing that Roger's strokes in the yonder were no less special than those on the ground. She was satisfied. And this was the problem.

For the first time in their nine-month relationship, while Roger toured the States prior to touring Germany as a guest of Udet, Melanie's needs were left in sexual limbo. Being of wealthy pampered stock, deprivation was something she knew not. After a thoughtful month, she called him and announced sadly that she was temporarily putting aside their relationship. Roger fell into deep depression. On a rainy night somewhere in the central part of the States, Roger thought of taking the '*hound* up beyond the oxygenless 12,000-foot mark; if he remained long enough he would become anoxic, and the '*hound* would tip over like a drugged puppy, and they would drill a formidable hole in the mid-section of America. It would be the aviator's way out.

Udet saved him.

He introduced Roger and his father to the famous Herman Goering, holder of the *Pour lé Merite*, World War I flying ace, friend of the Red Baron, future *Reichmarshal* of the Third Reich, sole recipient of the Grand Cross to the Knight's Cross, personal friend of Hitler, lover of aviation, admirer of aeronautical heroism, star of the Nuremberg trials, and crusher of the capsule cyanide. Enter Roger.

Goering was impressed. "The world of future aviation," he told Roger, "is in the hearts and souls of young men such as you. As long as we have hearts such as yours, aviation will never be in search of eagles."

Roger was stunned. Goering's swift, succinct, rousing words hit him like the beat of a war drum. He felt part of the ballast of aviation. The drop from 12,000 feet was no longer romantic. . . .

Now, the *Spitfire* came over the crowd of reporters again and drowned one of their questions.

Parker quietly pulled Cole off into the background. "Who the hell's flying that bastard?" he asked.

"Don't know, sir," Cole said.

"You get on the phone and call the limeys and tell 'em to get their asshole flyboy away

45

from my airbase or I'll blow the son-of-a-bitch right out of the sky." Cole disappeared into the building.

Griffin was enjoying a cigar now. He took questions with ease, tossed a couple of smiles at the cookies. After eight or nine minutes, Parker invited the group into a specially marked section in the Officers' Mess for a buffet lucheon. Preferred reporters sat next to Roger—Hamm from *Life*, with his photographer doing somersaults for good photo angles; Bob Len of *The New York Times*; Stout from Hearst scribbling frantically. Between bites other reporters sauntered over and shot Roger a few quickies. Two nurses got autographs and left smiles that promised heaven. Roger took names and noted the location of their quarters. One of the cooks, a short corporal with a puffy belly, said he'd seen Roger when he slipped into the magical loop, that he'd been a fan ever since. Could he shake Roger's hand and get a picture later? "Natch," Roger said, flashing his blue eyes. Meanwhile, Sutton was slouched in Parker's jeep watching the *Spitfire*.

Roger's picture and accompanying story would hit every major newspaper in America. One of the pictures would be erroneous; it showed Roger's porcelain-boned jaw jutting through a B-17's left hand window—the pilot's side—instead of the copilot's side of the ship. But the shot was a beauty. Roger, gazing into the heavens, presumably looking for nasty Germans. His cap was set back at a jaunty angle showing his white-blond hair, and he appeared prepared to take on the whole *Luftwaffe*. Melanie would have hers laminated and framed and would gaze at it for long periods of time, thinking about her honey-colored legs embracing Roger's strong back. *Life* did a spread, showing a few snaps of Roger at an early age; the day of his first solo; posing on loop day, as it was referred to; the Thompson Air Race; Roger in basic training posing behind a model of the B-17 he would soon fly.

Sutton watched the *Spitfire* gather speed. Engine tone went higher, and the spatula-shaped wings remained flat, glued level, showing the light gray underbelly, the oil cooler and wheelwells, the spent cartridge chutes, streaks of gunsmoke, oil smudges. A wide white band surrounded the fuselage just forward of the tailplane. The words, *The Borough of Lambeth*, were written in white block lettering behind the rust-colored exhaust stacks on the fighter's port side.

Sutton had been watching the *Spitfire* for ten minutes when the reporters, along with Griffin and Colonel Parker, came out of the mess hall.

Sutton focused on the spot in the sky and watched it grow into the *Spitfire*. The propeller was a disc of silver and the wings were thin, fragile-looking. It was fifty feet off the ground and coming directly at the crowd. When it swept over, it roared with air-cracking power.

"Bloody scary," Sutton heard one of the reporters say.

"Why's he doing that?" another asked Sutton.

"I don't know, but someone will stick his nose in a wringer for jerking around like that."

The *Spitfire*'s 26-year-old pilot tilted the nimble ship over on the left wing until it was perpendicular to the airfield. He circled the southern limit of the base and passed the end of the runway. The freshly painted insignia on the wing's surfaces were unseen. The pilot pulled down his goggles and nosed the ship over until the altimeter read less than 100 feet. He gave an extra tug on his shoulder harness and made sure the straps were as tight as he could bear. The wind, at fifteen knots, was from the north; and now he was flying into it, getting a crisp feel of the control surfaces. He'd flown this fighter a total of six hours and knew that it was a fast ship, light to the touch and very responsive, like a tuned sports car—so fast that, when throttled open, the pilot had to think ahead of every move, every motion of hand and foot, every impulse from brain to limb.

Ahead, framed in the frontpiece of the windscreen, Bassingbourn was a flat spread of runways and one-storied buildings cupped by grassy meadows and country roads. A sleepy-looking place. It was the way it appeared in the aerial photographs. On the hardstands, a few B-17s remained dormant: a fuel truck rolled down a taxiway; mechanics were working on engines. The pilot took a deep nervous breath and aimed the *Spitfire*'s spinner at a row of three parked B-17s.

The pilot was ready.

A simple quick correction on the control column brought the fighter lower as it zoomed back over the hedgelines it had passed moments ago. The young pilot was a half-mile away from Bassingbourn and he checked the gun switches again, to be certain. Sweat soaked his gloves, stained the blue-gray flight suit and trickled around his goggles and stung his cheeks. The plan was simple: he would make three high-speed passes, all very low, very fast. The first would be over the bombers, where the fuel truck was; the second would be over the ammunition dump; and the third over the runway at 100 feet—this one he would do inverted, so they could see the fresh insignias. This last one was an ego thing he had decided to do just ten minutes ago. Because if he was going to do this, take this chance, he wanted them to know who and what it was that had done this to them. It took nerve; a brazen aviator with a heart of steel. And he wanted recognition. The whole sweep, he'd estimated, would take less than ninety seconds.

He and the people on the ground would remember it for the rest of their lives.

At a distance of 600 yards from the bombers, his left hand pushed the throttle forward. His heart began to pound. The power surge forced his head, his torso, back into the headrest and seatback. His breathing was quick. Adrenalin pumped through his veins and his scrotum and sphincter muscles tightened. His heart beat through his temples.

The bombers filled the gunsight. His thumb moved over the firing button. He took one more deep breath. This was it. The end of the masquerade.

He waited one more second then committed himself.

The energy of his body, its force, seemed concentrated in the pad of his thumb as it crushed the firing button—as if the harder he pushed, pressed, the more power the bullets would have.

The eight .303s sang and the *Spitfire*'s body shuddered. The rounds exploded dirt and cement as their paths converged on the parked B-17s. They tore through metal and pierced the wings and ignited one of the bomber's fuel cells. As he swept over, one of the bombers exploded; a wingtip sprang into the air. He looked back and smiled and kept his fighter straight and level.

His name was August Baerenfaenger ("bearcatcher" in English) and he was a major in the *Luftwaffe*. A legend in Germany, he had eighty-eight enemy aircraft to his credit—which wasn't really that high by German standards. (Major Erich Hartman would end the war with an incredible 352 victories!) Baerenfaenger was known for his daring and, some said, his suicidal tendencies once strapped into an airplane

Generalfeldmarshal Hugo Sperrle, commander of *Luftflotte III*, had chosen Baerenfaenger ten days ago for this mission "so the world will know how brave the Reich's flyers are." *Luftflotte III's* operational sphere was eastern Britain and was stationed in northern France. Sperrle, as equally pompous as Goering, stationed himself in Paris at the luxurious *Palais de Luxembourg*—the one-time palace of Marie de Medicis. A man who refused to become familiar with the techniques of propaganda, Sperrle chose to use the Baerenfaenger mission as a demonstration of his willingness to appease Goering and to tell the world about the *Luftwaffe*.

Baerenfaenger, a beloved hero of the German people, was the perfect choice. He was already the proud holder of the Knight's Cross with Swords and Oakleaves, an award

Luftwaffe pilots referred to as the "tin tie" because it was worn around the neck. A short airman who could be mistaken for a jockey, today's feat would put him further up the ladder of celebrated German pilots. As he circled the *Spit* around for a second sweep he was already going down in history books.

He did a split-S and gained altitude for a sharper perspective of the target, then he dropped the nose again. He aimed the ship at the black column of smoke spiraling over the burning B-17. Figures were running for cover; people were clustered around the Officers' Mess. At an altitude of fifty feet his thumb pressed the firing button and held it for two three-second bursts. The airframe quivered. The fuel truck exploded and disappeared in a fireball; the wing of the other bomber began smoking. With precision, Baerenfaenger gently see-sawed the rudder pedals giving the .303s a wider spray range. The bullets shattered Plexiglass windows and tore through the skin of two more *Forts*. Spent shell casings from the Spitfire bounced off the cement runway, almost above the height of the fighter's wings. He waited two seconds then fired at the ammunition dump and watched the puffs of dirt as the bullets peppered the earth. The burst was too quick, ineffective, and there was insufficient time to concentrate on destroying the target.

There was chaos on the ground as Baeren-faenger knifed through the billowing smoke column and disappeared beyond the horizon's tree line. The controls responded perfectly as he tested them for damage. Then he tossed the fighter up vertically into the sky, climbing under full throttle. The powerful scream of the engine filled the countryside. He saw his face, a broad smile, reflected in the canopy. When he reached 1,000 feet he pulled back on the throttle and the engine popped and cracked through the hot exhaust stacks and the ship·fell over into a crisp hammerhead and dove for the earth. He was going back again.

Colonel Parker and the group of reporters were astounded. Parker's first reaction was that the *Spitfire* pilot had become enraged when told to stop horsing around and had taken revenge then somehow crashed somewhere on the base. Some of the reporters thought an accident had occurred. Parker refused to believe his eyes. The *Spitfire* he'd complained about was streaking over *his* airbase. Tongues of flame were shooting from eight spots on the wing's leading edges, trailing plumes of grey gunsmoke. *This is a reflection on me!* was Parker's first thought. *And it certainly won't help promotion.*

Len of the *Times* murmured, "I'll be a son-of-a-bitch."

The group watched the Bearcatcher's second sweep like Sunday airshow spectators.

"Traitor," someone barked.

"Unbelievable."

"Shit."

"Incredible."

Sutton laughed with admiration as he watched the *Spitfire* go into a steep vertical climb. "That's no traitor," he said. "That's one courageous German with a basket-sized pair of nuts, that's what that is."

"Bullshit!" roared Parker. "That's some crazy limey bastard."

Sutton reached into his pocket as he hopped off Parker's jeep. "A ten-dollar bill says he's a German pilot."

"You're on," Parker responded, "because that is absolutely preposterous. When he lands I'm going to have his ass strung up on Big Ben."

"When he lands, Colonel," said Sutton, admiring the fighter's ascent, "some German officer's going to give him a bottle of champagne and pin a medal on his ass."

Parker was incensed. "That's an asshole up there!" he shouted, pointing at the climbing dot. His body was shaking. Rag Tag scurried under Parker's jeep.

The Bearcatcher worked deftly. The ship came down like a falling arrow. At the last possible second he worked the controls and pulled out of the dive, once again hidden by the trees dotting the horizon. His body and the Spitfire were one, a scalpel ready to make one more cut. For a moment, from where the group stood, the plane's engine noise faded.

The third sweep over Bassingbourn would be the Bearcatcher's favorite. It was the optional razzle-dazzle part of the plan, the one Sperrle was hoping Baerenfaenger could accomplish.

After skimming tree tops and meadows for two miles, the Bearcatcher pulled the nose up to 100 feet, leveled off, and lined the ship up with the main runway.

"He's coming back!"

The plane was a black shape against hazy blue sky, a small venomous insect coming back for another kill blow.

A group of MPs began ineffectively firing at the plane with their .45 automatics.

At 210 MPH the Bearcatcher dazzled everyone.

At less than 100 feet above the runway he snapped the *Spitfire* over onto its back. A line of sooty exhaust smoke marked the flight path.

"He's insane."

"Wow!"

"Oh. . . ."

Len stood with his hands on his hips shaking his head.

Griffin's blue eyes blinked disbelievingly.

Sutton smiled.

Gunfire popped in the distance.

A quarter of the way down the runway

Baerenfaenger wobbled the *Spit*'s wings and gave the crowd some German razzmatazz.

"Nice," Sutton said softly. "Very . . . nice." He drew the *very* out an extra second, almost singing it in praise of the pilot.

Hamm from *Life* agreed and continued shouting instructions to his photographer: "Are you getting this! Christ! I hope you're getting this!"

Before Baerenfaenger reached the end of the runway he hit full-throttle and the *Spitfire* snapped over with a motion of exquisite perfection. A pilot's delight. And August Baerenfaenger knew it. He screamed out the battle cry of all German pilots, *"Horrido!"*—the word used in greeting or in parting among comrades of the *Luftwaffe*.

"Beautiful. Really outstanding," Sutton said, impressed with the *Spitfire*'s performance and the pilot's obvious courage.

The fighter climbed vertically and suddenly everyone knew why the pilot performed this dramatic, spectacular escape. The engine bellowed and reverberated off the ground as the aircraft continued gaining altitude, straining for clear blue sky.

On the topsides of the wings, where the British roundels had once been, the sun caught two freshly painted German crosses.

Parker lost his bet.

CHAPTER FOUR

A half hour after the *Spitfire* disappeared, Sutton was standing at a relaxed position of attention in front of Colonel Parker's desk. He'd been standing silently like this for the past five minutes.

The phone had rung twice, and Sergeant Cole appeared three times—once to bring in Sutton's file, and once to escort Rag Tag into the office.

"Make yourself comfortable, Captain," Parker finally said. He was draped over his chair like a sack of laundry. "I understand you had a bit of a nasty time over Metz today."

"Yes, sir. I lost eight men."

"Also, Doc Matlin told me you're reluctant about your transfer to my Group. Is that correct?"

"Yes, sir, it is."

"Why?"

"May I be blunt, Colonel?"

"Go ahead, Captain."

57

Sutton looked into Parker's eyes. "You've got a reputation, Colonel. You drive your men without thinking about them, about their feelings. It seems you only care about yourself and your own ambitions in the Air Force. I don't think I'd like to work for a man like that. Also, I didn't ask for this transfer—it was just handed to me yesterday."

Parker could've been a lizard or a fish in a previous life because he wore those steel-rimmed glasses that made him look like he was constantly sucking air, looking for a bug to devour. His desk was a tribute to himself—West Point photos, a hole-in-one golf ball, a photo with General Eaker, a small framed display of previous insignia of rank, his name carved in a block of marble, that sort of thing.

He unfolded his arms and stretched a hand out for Sutton's folder and sat in silence for a while. Sutton, without asking, plopped down in a chair next to the desk and the phone rang.

"Well?"

Drops of rain ticked the window and the sky was turning lead gray. Parker was the type who was hated by everyone below him and loved by everyone above. Those below knew he'd step on them to move upward. Superiors cared little about what tactics he employed to accomplish their orders, and there would certainly be a general's star waiting for him in the near future. He would've made a good corporate vice president if that was his choosing.

Sutton heard Cole's squeky voice on the receiver. He was reporting the *Lazy Lady's* damage (it was a total wreck); the effect of the bombing run over Metz; and the whereabouts of the reporters. Cole was proficient at obtaining morsels of information like this. He was Parker's palace spy, his man Friday. He would sulk around the base with stooped shoulders and had an ear like a radar dish for barracks gossip. A tidbit for Parker was praise for Cole. He was Parker's major domo—when he entered rooms they would go dead with silence.

"I can't see him right now. Tell him I'm sorry."

Someday someone would reach across Parker's desk and squash him like an insect.

"No. I'll handle that matter myself, Sergeant."

He put the phone down and looked at the folder again and he said: "Now, Captain, let me ask you again. Why don't you want to fly for me?"

"I told you—it's really nothing personal. I just don't like the way you run your men."

Parker's eye twitched. He reached down and stroked Rag Tag's neck. "You know something, Jim boy. I take care of this animal." His Midwestern drawl grew thick. "I feed him, I make him feel loved. I make sure he's comfortable. I even get him laid once in a while. And one of the reasons I like him is because, unlike most pilots in this group, he doesn't give me any sass. When he does, I slap him down hard." He leaned over the desk and folded his arms. "I don't take back-talk from any of my pilots, and I demand loyalty and respect. Get my drift, Captain?" He expected Sutton to say something—and that's why Sutton remained silent. Parker said, "Things are really very simple here. Everyone does their job and no one gets their peter stuck in a propeller. And, I might add, I certainly hope yours is latched on tight." The colonel gave a dreary smile.

He'd been in command six months and when other Group commanders would lean back, Parker would push beyond what was expected. He tapped Sutton's folder with one of his spidery fingers. "You see, Captain, I've been handed a special top-secret mission, and you've been chosen to fly it. You've got fourteen missions to your credit. You're an expert at flying low-level missions, and the mission that's shaping up will require a man just like you. And I've assembled a special crew for you to command."

Sutton's eyebrows arched, and his brown eyes showed curiosity. "What kind of mission is it?"

"It's top secret."

"Oh for God's sakes that's not what I mean."

Parker pressed back into his chair. "I can't divulge it now. It's highly classified and we're still working out the details." He drummed the blotter with his thin fingers, keeping a steady beat going while Sutton thought about what he said.

"I'm thinking about it."

"Don't. You have no choice. You either take this mission or face a court-martial. Up till now, Captain, you've busted every rule in the book. Wing has a list of discrepancies on you as long as your arm. Look, this mission came up a few days ago and the first man picked was you. You were highly recommended. That's why they transferred you to my Group. We've been assigned this mission and you're going to fly it."

"I said I'd give it some thought."

"You can't!" Parker slammed his fist on the desk. "You have no choice."

"All right," he said. "but in the meantime I want something from you."

"Good," said Parker.

Sutton sat up straight. "I'll fly," he said, leaning toward the desk, "but in the meantime, I want you to process a transfer for me. You see, I don't believe in you or your methods."

The blood drained from Parker's face. His knuckles turned white. "I don't understand you, Captain."

"There's not much to understand, Colonel. You've said things were simple. I'll fly for you because I love to fly. I'll be part of your secret mission. But after that, I want to be transferred out of your Group."

Parker said nothing. This could cause trouble. If Sutton expressed himself to Wing, the whole matter could be blown out of proportion and Parker's career could be jeopardized. A whole career could be shattered because of a disgruntled captain.

Sutton lit a cigarette. "I'll put it in writing if my verbal request isn't sufficient."

"No need for that," Parker shot back. "Look, Captain, we've got some big missions coming up and the 45th needs you. This mission will be a real challenge for you."

"In the meantime, get the transfer rolling."

"These things take time, you know." Parker's hands were sweating. He pressed a button and Sergeant Cole appeared. "Captain Sutton here would like a transfer. I've agreed to it after he flies for us. Make out the necessary forms. I'll sign them when they're complete." Cole left the room. "In the meantime, Captain, you're under my command."

Sutton nodded. He couldn't see how anyone, a child, an insect, Rag Tag, could stand to share the same air with Parker. When he spoke to you in a group or at a party, Parker was one of those people that would glance around the room for someone of higher stature. He held himself in such high esteem that he did not listen to or acknowledge anyone else—unless he needed to use him for something. Then he'd put on the kid gloves and look the man straight in the eye.

"Get me Griffin's folder," Parker said into the intercom. "And tell Sergeant Holden that I'll have a crew down there to check out that new ship that's coming in. Tell him that Captain Sutton's the new aircraft commander and that he'll be down there shortly."

"Griffin?" Sutton said.

"He's your new copilot."

"Oh shit. He's a three-dollar phony, an ego-maniac."

"Haven't you heard of the famous Roger Griffin."

"Yes, and that's why I'm telling you he's a first-class phony."

"He's a good stunt pilot."

"Colonel, in case you haven't noticed, the B-17 isn't a stunt plane. It's about as agile as an overloaded bus."

Parker sat upright in his chair and placed his pale fingers flat on the desk. He hated being cornered like this.

He said slowly, "Captain, I don't care much for your attitude. You might as well know that. Nor do I care much for what you think of me. I know you dislike me, but, you see, I'm mud-proof. I've been spat on by people who've had bigger balls than you could ever dream of owning. And so that you know how I feel about you, let me say that I think you are an unorthodox pilot, that you march to a different drummer. Perhaps that is why you're an excellent pilot. And that is precisely the reason why you've been chosen for this mission and why you're going to remain a member of the 45th. So that you can do your job—"

"And make you look good in the process."

"Maybe I've been mistaken about you. Maybe it's that attitude of yours that gets you out of bed each morning. I do know, too, that you are a disrespectful officer, that your demeanor is less than proper, and that what you should do once this war's over is to get your raggedy ass out of the Air Force. You are indeed a paradox, and I suggest that if it weren't for your impressive flying record I would do everything, along with the other people you've flown for, to dismiss you. There have been times, Captain, when you've proven to be an outright embarrassment to the Air Force. I shall do everything I can to effect your transfer after this mission is flown. In the meantime, if you step out of line just once, I will step on you." He squeezed Rag Tag's neck and the dog yelped.

Sutton squashed his cigarette out then stood in front of Parker's desk. He said, "It's refreshing to hear such honesty from a man who's normally full of bullshit."

Parker returned Sutton's salute. He said, curtly, "I want you to go and find your aircraft and introduce yourself to your new crew."

"Yes, *sir*."

When the door closed behind Sutton, Parker buzzed Cole and in a few seconds he appeared.

"Yes, sir?" Cole said.

"Did you type up Sutton's transfer?"

"Yes, sir, I just—"

"Tear it up."

Cole smiled.

CHAPTER FIVE

The morning sky began to clear.

Earlier, it had been filled with rain, and now smudges of long, gray-blue clouds swept the horizon. Above them to the west, orange-red light smeared the skyline where the sun's disc shone, a brilliant bloodstone burning a black Atlantic. The rain had rolled west; and to the east, a few scattered clouds swept swiftly to the southwest. The smell of fresh water was everywhere, and the grass sparkled emerald-silver.

Rivulets of rain water dripped steadily from the long wings of a factory-fresh B-17. A group of nine airmen stood talking below the number one engine. They'd been here for ten minutes; they were told earlier to report here to meet their new aircraft commander, Capt. James Sutton.

Bush and Skolinsky told the others that they'd flown a couple of missions.

"Lucky guys," Rowe the bombardier said. His tone was negative, and the others noted it. Rowe was moody, introspective. The day before his first mission three months ago, he'd had a feeling he'd never complete the mandatory twenty five raids. He had dreams about this. It was always the same one: *The nose of the ship takes a direct hit and disintegrates and he falls from twenty-five thousand feet without his parachute, which is shredded from the explosion. He keeps falling, pulling the D-ring as he tumbles helplessly through the frigid air. The D-ring is immovable. He sweeps his hand quickly around his back searching for the familiar shape of the pack. Only ribbons remain, bannering in the slipstream of his body as he drops 120 miles per hour. He is an organism formed by flesh and blood waiting to splatter into infinity. He realizes he is mortal, that he will die, that everything will end. As he falls he looks down once and his body fills with ineffable horror. Terror! He sees the bombers pass overhead, their small silhouettes marked by chalky contrails against the white glare of cold blue sky. He reaches up, tries to grab one, to hang from it. But he can't. He keeps falling!*

Each time he wakes he's soaked in perspiration. He'd had the dream so many times—like a repetitive movie—that is had become reality, something that he experienced physically. He hadn't told anyone, and he was certain that this would be the way he would die—falling from his ship without his chute. As the men talked, Rowe wondered where he'd find the courage to fly another mission.

Sgt. Sam Whitefeather stood most of the time staring at the aircraft. He checked for flaws the way only a veteran crewman would—through intuition and gut feeling. He didn't like the looks of this new ship.

The navigator, Bob Gibson, was in a light mood. Last night he won three hundred dollars in a poker game. He had the money—three, one-hundred-dollar bills—folded neatly in the right pocket of his flying jacket. Occasionally, he felt them, and this brought a smile to his face. Unlike Rowe, Gibson felt very lucky. Since his first mission he was certain he'd get home alive.

There was only one other crewman more certain of this—Benny Tutone, flight engineer and turret gunner.

He was telling everyone about a woman he slept with in London a week ago: the positions, what she said, how she moaned; everything was graphically conveyed through his quick Brooklyn accent. Rowe shook his head as he listened. Tutone, he thought, was so filled with energy and motion that he would overload someday, like a fuse, and explode.

Kid Kiley, the tail gunner, was so young looking, so frail in appearance, that there was an investigation going on at Wing to determine what his real age was. He didn't look more than fourteen. He had a choirboy's face, a thin layer of blond fuzz for a beard. He'd won the Distinguished Flying Cross and two Purple Hearts; he had four German fighters to his credit. Three were confirmed kills, the other a probable — which he had to share with the turret gunner from Captain Chrisp's ship, who swore the fighter was his alone, not the Kid's. After the mission, the Kid called the turret gunner a motherfucker and knocked a tooth out of his mouth. Chrisp witnessed the event, reported it to Parker, and added that the Kid looked too young to be in the Air Force. This started the investigation. Since then, the Kid referred to everyone in Chrisp's crew as motherfuckers. He was Irish-Catholic, from Boston, and this was the stiffest word in his vocabulary. He never cursed except when he spoke of Chrisp and his crew. "Collectively and individually," he had said, "they are motherfuckers of the first order." No one disputed him. The Chrisp crew were a bunch of egotistical favorites of Colonel Parker's — particularly Chrisp himself.

The new B-17 was flown to Bassingbourn from Long Beach, California by the WAACS — the Women's Army Air Corps Service. The pilot, a 23-year-old first lieutenant from Nevada, was an auburn-haired woman built like a statue — tight and long. She had hazel eyes and a pair of breasts that made men utter obscenities through panting

69

breath. She had ferried more planes—B-17s, P-38s, P-47s, P-39s, B-24s—than the huddled crew had seen collectively in their lifetimes. Her name was Trisha Reed, and people called her "T.R.," which she loved because, she said, "it's got a spiffy ring to it." She had been flying since she was twelve; before she had her driver's license, before her first date, before her first kiss.

Despite her sultry eyes, dark complexion, high-boned cheeks, T.R. was still *virgo intacto*. No man had touched her iron-flat belly, grazed her silky thighs, or entwined one little finger through her virgin forest. T.R. was indeed pristine, waiting to be hit by a thunderbolt before she parted her lean legs. She loved men, but no one would touch her until she genuinely loved him. Until then, flying was all that mattered.

And she did not merely fly airplanes—she manhandled them, became part of their bodies, grasped them, stroked them, choked them, banged them, cursed them, kicked them, loved them, and strapped them tightly onto her back. "Some girls have great legs," she confided to a friend. "but I've got a real peach of a back." Obviously T.R. was looking the wrong way in the mirror. Some said she knew how to talk airplane, that she could stare one down for a minute and know if it was ripe or sour. When she climbed aboard, she was part of the ship; like the cables or the metal. Its skin was her skin, its wings her arms, its legs her legs, its paint her makeup. She was the pearl inside the oyster.

She dropped through the forward hatch then heaved her duffel bag over her shoulder.

"This is a damned good ship," she said, chucking her thumb up toward the nose section. "What it needs is a good crew, and you guys look like the sorriest bunch of bananas I've ever seen. But this snake sure flies pretty. You guys assigned to this bird?"

"Yes," Griffin said, "We're waiting for the pilot."

"What's his name?" asked T.R.

"Captain Sutton," Bush said.

She grinned and looked at the group. "Old hotshot Charlie, huh? Big Jim Sutton. Well, you guys got yourselves one hell of a pilot. Jim kicks ass and doesn't give a damn about rules, but he sure can fly a bird. Matter of fact, I thought they were drumming him out of the Air Force. If any of you guys know him, you know he's prime cut. A little rough around the curves, but you guys are really lucky because Jim can take a ship like this and turn snap-rolls inside a box of corn flakes."

"Seems like you know a lot about flying," Griffin said, flashing his sky-blue eyes at T.R.

"Know some, that's true."

Griffin extended his hand. "My name's Griffin. Roger Griffin. I'm sure you've heard of me." He was beaming, hoping for recognition from this attractive girl.

"Griffin?" She thought for a second. "You the guy that did the loop?"

"That's me."

Her eyes caught the fading rose light and her skin shone buff-colored. She gave Griffin a broad smile and showed a row of perfect white teeth. A breeze hooked her hair over her eye, and there was a moment of silence. Then she said: "The loop coulda been better. I saw it on Movietone."

Roger appeared hurt. "What are you doing tomorrow night?"

T.R. glanced at her Gruen wristwatch. "I might be at the Officers' Club." As she turned, a jeep slipped to a halt nearby.

"How 'bout a date?" Griffin asked.

"If I'm there, I'm there. If I'm not, I'm not."

Sutton got out of the jeep and helped T.R. toss her duffel bag into the back. They spoke for a minute then the jeep pulled away.

He introduced himself to the waiting airmen. After opening a manila folder, he slipped out a double-spaced typewritten sheet of paper.

"First," he said, "I want you to know that I think you guys are the biggest group of screw-offs flying in the Air Force. And whether you know it or not, that's why Parker's assembled us. I want you to know that if you screw around once while I'm your aircraft commander, I will personally kick your ass from one end of that ship to another. I will make it so damned tough for you you'll wish you never put on a uniform. Now, who's Sergeant Bush?"

Bush moved forward. "I am, sir."

"Do you know why you were assigned to me?"

"No, sir. But we heard a rumor about a secret mission."

"The rumor," Sutton said, "is now verified as correct and true. And you, Sergeant Bush, have been assigned to it because no one else stuck his hand in the air when they were looking for a second waist gunner.

"I think I'm capable, sir."

"We'll find out soon enough."

Sutton's thick brown hair fluttered in the breeze and he checked the sheet again. "Skolinsky—ditto for you. Inexperienced but capable."

"Yes, sir. I think I'll do okay, and I'm anxious to fly for you."

"Okay ain't good enough. A lot of guys do *okay* and they get killed. The Germans love guys who do *okay*. They have 'em for breakfast and fart 'em out in the afternoon."

"Then I'll do better than okay, sir."

The thirty-year-old Rowe was next on the list, the oldest man in the crew, a career officer who'd been in the Air Force thirteen years and had been busted five times. He'd made major once but got drunk one night and destroyed a bar. Sergeants and privates that Rowe knew when he enlisted were now lieutenant colonels and colonels. One was a brigadier general. He dreaded combat so much he drank to forget it. A ladies' man, Rowe had a fear of getting shot in the groin. While most men flew with one flak jacket, Rowe flew with four—one around his torso in the standard manner, one over his groin, and two stacked under the appendage he feared losing. Because of his background, Parker "volunteered" him for this crew and for the big mission.

"Where'd you get the nickname *Deadeye* from, Rowe?" Sutton asked.

"Because I'm a good bombardier."

"Bullshit."

"Well, I'd rather not talk about it."

Sutton remembered. He told the crew, "Rowe got loaded and brought an English friend back on base with him one afternoon and took him out to a B-17. He told the Englishman that he was a bombardier, and how great he was at his work. So the Englishman asked for a demonstration, because he was boozed up, too. Rowe asked what kind of demonstration, and the Englishman challenged him to piss in a bucket from the wingtip of the plane they were standing under. The only problem was, the bet was made on open-house day and there were a lot of proper English ladies walking around. Right, Rowe?"

Rowe looked hurt.

"Did you win the bet?" asked Bush.

Tutone said, "Shit, no. He didn't even get it over the edge."

"That," Rowe said, "was the embarrassing part."

"Well, Lieutenant," Sutton said, looking down at the sheet again, "if you try that again you're going to be pissing into a stiff breeze." He ran his finger under Sam Whitefeather's name. He said, "What didn't you like about Captain Chrisp, Chief?"

The Chief shifted his weight and stuffed his hands into his leather flight jacket. There was warmth in his deep black eyes and his voice was rich and clear, the words precise. "Captain Chrisp is a man who doesn't know which end his ass is hung on."

"I suppose," said Sutton, "that one of the problems you had with him was that you told him which end."

"Correct."

Next on the list was the radio operator, "Bo" Baker, a 24-year-old corporal from Rhode Island. He'd completed twenty two missions and had three remaining before his tour was completed. Three days ago, his bomber was hit over France and disintegrated after fire broke out over the English Channel. He was the only crewman to bail out safely. An avid reader, he was almost through with Richard Llewellyn's *How*

Green Was My Valley. He was pensive, a loner. With only three missions remaining, he distrusted every pilot in the Group, including Sutton, who would be in charge of his life until he reached the magic number, 25. Lately, his feelings about pilots were no secret.

"I know how you feel," Sutton said coldly, "but I can't do a damned thing about it. Parker apparently doesn't like your attitude."

He glanced at the sheet again. "Kiley!" he called out.

"Here, sir."

"The investigation into your age should be completed soon. The Air Force thinks," Sutton said, looking at the group, "that Kiley here lied about his age in order to get into the Air Force."

"That sure ain't the facts, sir. I told 'em the truth when I enlisted."

"Not only that," Sutton said, "but Parker doesn't like anyone calling Chrisp and his boys motherfuckers. That's why we've been honored with Kiley's presence."

"Worst thing that can happen," said Tutone, "is that you don't get to shoot at Germans. That's the worst thing."

Gibson the navigator was next. "Lieutenant Gibson's been around a while," said Sutton. "The only problem is he doesn't want to fly anymore. But Irontail Parker convinced him he should do otherwise. Gibson has the distinction of having bailed out of three B-17s—once in the Channel, twice over France. His most outstanding achievement is slugging an officer in the face."

Bush was impressed with this. "Did you get hurt?"

"When I bailed out or when I hit the officer?"

"When you bailed out."

"Yeah. I was killed the last time."

Everyone laughed, but it was partially true. He'd been missing for ten days and was presumed killed in action. His belongings were packed together by Sergeant Cole and a telegram was sent to his parents. The day after it arrived, Gibson appeared at Bassingbourn. He had four Purple Hearts and the Distinguished Flying Cross.

"Last and not least," Sutton said softly, "is the illustrious Roger Griffin. Just ask him and he'll tell you."

"He already has," Tutone mumbled. Everyone grinned because they had Griffin pegged as a braggart.

He showed a nice smile, a row of immaculate teeth. He took a step forward and said, "I'm not so sure I like your attitude, Captain."

"Then you can leave right now. You see, gentlemen, Roger here was the only man to volunteer for this crew, for the secret mission. Lieutenant, I can assure you this ain't going to be as easy as the loop." Sutton was tempted to tell him that he'd test-flown the Aerohound before Roger performed the publicity-grabbing loop. "You've got to learn something, buddy," Sutton said, facing Griffin squarely, "this war ain't a three-ring circus with you in the middle. Keep that in mind next time someone snaps your picture."

Roger took a step back. He already hated Sutton; he knew the captain's reputation, and no one had ever talked to him like that. He was Roger Griffin for Christ's sakes and no one spoke to a Griffin like that. But he kept his mouth shut.

"All right," Sutton said, putting the sheet back into the folder. "This is the crew. I don't care whether you like me or each other, but we're going to fly together because we have a job to do. And we're going to do it my way. We've been assembled for a special mission. Either because you're good, or because you're a bunch of misfits and they don't give a damn if we succeed or fail. Maybe they want to keep their favorites for safer raids, I don't know. I want you here tomorrow at 0800 hours. We're going to get into that turkey and get acquainted. Any questions?"

"Captain," Whitefeather said, "before you arrived, we were wondering about this ship." He pointed to the B-17.

"What about it?"

"Well, first of all, it looks like shit. And

second, we're not too anxious about flying in her." The plane had an unusual camouflage scheme: blotches of dark-green sprayed over a base of olive-drab. It was the only such scheme in the Group. But it had been ordered this way at the factory because the scheme would aid them in their secret mission.

"It's an experimental paint job, Chief," Sutton said. "And I hear it's part of what we're going to be using her for. So, you better get used to it."

"Sure looks awful," Rowe added.

"Look," Sutton said, annoyed, "I don't care if it looks like cattle crap, what matters is how it flies. It just came from the factory. Come here," he said to the Chief. The crew followed him to the fuselage near the port waist gun window. "Stick your nose to it, Chief, and take a good whiff."

"Smells like fresh paint."

"Smells like bird shit," Rowe said, taking a deep breath.

"There's no doubt," said the blue-eyed Griffin, trying to sound like an expert on aircraft, "that this is a brand-new ship. I've visited the Long Beach factory a couple of times and that place smells just like this—fresh paint, clean grease, and new rubber." He turned, looked at the Chief. "Believe me, Sergeant, I know what I'm talking about."

"That don't mean she can fly." the Chief

replied. Before he got into a bomber, before he put his life on the line, he had to be certain that his plane wasn't a lemon. The others felt the same, and the Chief was expressing their opinion. He knew the plane was fresh from the factory. But to him, as well as the others, it didn't look right with all those blotches. The Chief needed proof before he felt content. He had to know everything about her: where she was made, what date and time. If there was a kink, a flaw anywhere in her sleek body, he and the others had to know. Before they bought it, they wanted the bloodline.

Aside from Sutton and Griffin, Tutone was the only crewman that seemed satisfied with the new ship. "Chief, what would you rather have," he asked, "a broad that looked good and humped bad, or a broad that humped good and looked bad?"

"A good-looking humper."

"Well, handsome son of Sitting Bull," Tutone said, slamming his boot against the tire, "you got it right here! A good-lookin' humper. Take it from me, Benny Tutone, the world's greatest living aerial gunner! This is a class-A bird." He kicked the tire again. "I can feel it! I can sense it in my gunner's bones. *This is a peach!*"

Gibson and Rowe applauded. "Bravo!"

Sutton checked his watch. "All right. Any more hotshot questions?"

There were none.

The crew snapped to attention and saluted.

CHAPTER SIX

The Chief was the first to arrive the next morning. He sat crosslegged on the grass, a hundred yards off the port wing of the ship he mistrusted. A seasonal breeze furled his night-black hair. His broad shoulders, muscular and bow-shaped, were hunched over his powerful thighs. The solid, square jaw jutted out defiantly, and his deep black eyes peered at the airplane like a hunter scrutinizing fresh prey. At twenty four, the Chief's sunwashed face had aged long ago. It was an old map of wisdom and dignity, brushed with lines of courage handed down from generations of enduring ancestors. A proud man, the Chief knew the importance of listening to intuition, the need for instinct. But now he was troubled, filled with doubt. Inside, there was a voice he was waiting to hear from; a voice that would pass judgment on the creature sitting dormant at the end of his stare. When it would come to him, it would be decisive and it would have more credibility than Tutone's impulsive answer yesterday. Only then could the Chief and the others fly aboard her with confidence. This had been the Chief's way, and that was why Chrisp hated him—because he relied on something spiritual, something from the heart. It was something Chrisp could not understand.

Forty-five minutes ago, twenty B-17s had taken off. But the Chief was oblivious to the growl of their engines. He had been here almost an hour, mesmerized, chain-smoking half a pack of Lucky Strikes. As he smoked, the ship's crew chief, Sergeant Holden, directed the maintenance crew prepping the bomber for flight.

The Chief lit another smoke.

"The beast," he whispered. He stood and inhaled and said the words again: "The beast." The cigarette fell to the grass and the Chief jogged to the airplane. He stopped at the large tire on the main landing gear and slammed his boot against the rubbery object, giving it more energy than Tutone had done yesterday.

"That's your new name—*The Beast!*"

The ship was unofficially baptized. It didn't matter that the others hadn't given their approval, that the aircraft commander hadn't agreed. With force and power, the Chief had decided that there would be no alternative name.

The Beast. That was the name of this new B-17.

Since he had led most of the crew to believe that there could be something amiss in her bones, he could do likewise and lead them to accept the name he'd just chosen. He was convinced of that.

Sergeant Holden saw the Chief's sacrilegious blow to his new aircraft. He jumped down from the forward hatch and walked quickly toward the Chief. He had a cigar stump stuck in the corner of his mouth. Some said it was the same cigar he bought in basic training ten years ago, and that he slept with it, too. The cigar was never lit but remained like a jagged blossom, a permanent feature of his bald head.

"What the hell are you doing kicking that tire like that?" he asked.

"Checking the tire pressure."

"Bullshit."

"Yeah, I am. It's about two pounds off."

"The air pressure's fine. It's your brain that's off."

"How do you know."

"Because, asshole, I checked the tire out with this." Holden held up a silver pressure gauge and wagged it in the Chief's eyes.

"How do you know anything's good on this heap?"

"How do I know? Well, I'll tell you. I know the same way I know if anything's good on you—and that's by inserting this up the ass, that's how."

The Chief faced the intimidating Holden

squarely, faking a few jabs around his shoulders. "Look, I got to fly in this witch and before I get in I got to know as much as I can. I'm not getting into a cursed bomber. Now, you want to make something out of it—let's go."

Holden waved his gauge. It was his wand, his baton, his symbol of office. "This airplane ain't cursed, jackass. This bird's checked out. All you have to do is get your ticket punched at the gate, take a seat, and when the time comes, shoot your little popgun. And the next time I see you haulin' off and smackin' *my* tire like I just seen you, I'm going to lift it and drop it on your dumb head."

"You ain't doing shit," the Chief said. He backed off a step. He knew he was in enemy territory; Holden's men were watching the action. The Chief knew this was Holden's domain, that the maintenance and repair of this $185,000 aircraft was his and his alone. And like most mechanics, Holden resented anyone poking their noses into his business. Kicking the ship was kicking Holden—a disagreeable but hardworking and industrious man who disliked pilots and crewmen. They were the main source of broken and malfunctioning equipment. If he had his way, he'd repair the plane and let it sit there as a museum piece, dusting it off periodically. When a crew returned a shot-up bomber, inevitably Holden would stomp around in anger—not at the Germans, but at the crew for allowing *his* ship to get mauled in such a manner.

A truck wheeled around and halted in front of the plane's nose, and the crew spilled out. Tutone took the lead, walking quickly, a child anxious for the merry-go-round ride. He shouted, "Hey, Chief! Are you ready to fly?"

The Chief gave him a cold stare.

"Well?" asked Tutone, "what do you guys think? Do we have a good bird or don't we?"

Holden slipped his pressure gauge into his overall pocket. "You have a mighty good bird," he said, "and don't let the Chief spook you."

"Terrific," Tutone said, looking at the crew. "That's what I like to hear. You hear that, guys—this ship's okay."

They were dressed in flight suits, leather flying helmets with large goggles, Mae West inflatable life vests, and flying gloves. Griffin wore a long silk scarf. All of them wore buttoned-up shirts and regulation ties. No one looked enthusiastic except Tutone.

"Sir," the Chief said to Sutton. "I've got a request."

"What is it?"

"I thought up a name for the ship. I'd like to know if it's all right if we name her *The Beast?*"

"*The Beast?*" Sutton thought for a couple of seconds, looking at the faces of the crew.

"What do you guys think?"

Most of them didn't care.

Griffin said it sounded all right, looking at the blotches again.

Rowe shrugged his shoulders. "Why not."

Kid Kiley said nothing. He was waiting for the general opinion to develop.

Bo Baker said: "Don't mean a hill of beans to me."

"I don't like it," Tutone said. His enthusiasm had vanished.

"How 'bout we name it after your momma," Gibson said to Tutone, hoisting his bag up through the hatch.

Tutone shot back at him: "You know, Lieutenant, with all due respect, sir, for a guy who pissed off an airplane's wing, I wouldn't go talkin' 'bout a guy's mother."

"What would you like to call her?" Bush asked Sutton.

"*The Beast* is fine," he said, tossing his gear in after Gibson's.

"When we get back today," the Chief said, "we'll have *The Beast* drawn on the nose section."

"All right," said Sutton, heaving himself into the hatch, "let's get going. The train's leaving in five minutes."

When a B-17 sat idle for more than two hours, the normal procedure was to have the propellers turned over by the crew. Three complete revolutions had to be made before the engines were started. While this was done, Griffin and Sutton were in the cockpit checking the weight and balance data. They went over forms F and AN01-1-40. Sutton moved his hands over the switches and controls and read the items off the preflight checklist. Every switch, every control, had to be set and determined correct before startup began. Starting the four engines was a complex procedure. The series of switches, controls, valves, and so on had to be ordered up before the props turned.

The emergency ignition switch was on and the master battery switches were on. Hydraulic pump switches were turned on and the turbo controls were moved to "off." All fuel shut-off valves were opened, then the throttle was cracked to 1,000 RPM. Cowl flaps were opened and the return valves were set in the locked position. The fire extinguisher valve was set to the number one engine. Griffin was directed to turn the carburetor air filters to "on." The mixture controls were set to "engine off." Primers were set to the "off" position, and the number three fuel booster pump was started. Intercooler controls were moved to "cold."

"All right, Griffin," Sutton said, "we're going to fly a real airplane now. Fire up the number one engine."

Griffin moved the start switch to the number one engine and energized it for twelve seconds. He knew he was being watched carefully; he did everything by the book. After twelve seconds, while the start switch was held, he threw the mesh switch. Then, with four quick strokes, he primed the cylinders, atomizing the primer charge. The engine gulped, coughed, spit blue smoke, then roared. Prop blades whirled in the sunlight. The procedure was repeated for each engine.

Griffin checked the gauges. "We've got fifty pounds per square inch on the oil pressure." This was a signal for Sutton to raise the RPMs to 1,250 to get readings off the instruments.

Fuel pressure climbed to the prescribed 16 PSI, and the oil pressure rested at 80. The oil temp had risen to 191 degrees and the cylinder head temp was at a normal 400. The engine and accessories ground test was performed. Griffin checked to be certain that the doors and hatches were secured.

"Pilot to ball gunner," Sutton said into the interphone throat microphone, "secure the lower turret and point your guns rearward."

The ganged propeller controls on the center console were set for high RPM and locked. Griffin made certain the battery switches were on and the hydraulic switch was in auto. Then he checked the warning lights: tail wheel unlocked—red; landing gear—green; vacuum—off. Fuel quantities were satisfactory.

The command radio was turned on and

the flight controls were checked. Sutton contacted the control tower for clearance and signaled Sergeant Holden to remove the wheel chocks. With the mixture controls in the automatic rich, he checked the ignition at 1,900 and 2,000 RPM, making certain that it didn't rise by more than 100. Each engine was run up individually and the type B-2 General Electric turbosupercharger controls were adjusted for forty six inches manifold pressure. The turbosuperchargers were controlled by automatic hydraulic regulators adjusted from the pilot's control pedestal.

While Sutton worked through this procedure, Griffin checked the fuel pressure, oil pressure, oil temp and cylinder temp gauges, then he turned the fuel boost pumps on.

The trim tabs were set in neutral and both pilots closed their windows. With the inboard throttles locked, Sutton goosed the outboard throttle forward and *The Beast* began to roll. Holden flashed an uncharacteristically sharp salute, which Sutton returned.

The Hamilton standard three-bladed props, which were hydromatically controlled with constant-speed and full-feathering provisions, cracked the air. Holden's chest vibrated with the pulse of the four Wright, nine-cylinder radial engines.

Should engine control cables be shot away, four of the controls will automatically assume predetermined positions: throttles, wide open; superchargers, 65% power; intercoolers, cold;

and propellers, 1850 RPM. Functioning of the automatic control at one unit will not affect placement of controls at other units, or of similar controls on other engines.

The Beast hesitated under the power surge then rolled off the hardstand.

Tutone was in the engineer's position between Griffin and Sutton; he could feel his stomach tingle with excitement; the hair on his neck bristled. "Soon," he said, "we're gonna find out how good this meatball can fly."

Sutton was always a little tight in the groin before takeoff, until he was clear of the runway and at a safe altitude. When he was younger, when he'd begun to fly, he thought this feeling would disappear with experience. But it never did. Somehow he liked the feel of anxiety because it kept him alert. Little disasters, big disasters: they all ran through his mind between startup and takeoff. Nothing mattered except four good engines.

"So far so good," Tutone said.

"We'll see."

"It will be a silky takeoff," Griffin said. He was trying to impress them with his confidence and his ability, but they saw through it.

The Beast reached the end of the runway and Sutton wheeled it around. He turned the generator switch on.

"Here we go. Hang on to your jocks."

He opened the ganged throttles and took

four seconds going up to the "full" position. Tutone grinned when he felt the power surge and saw Sutton smile, the sunlight catching his brown eyes, showing delight, a love for flying. The Wrights were beating out full power.

The bomber rolled down the runway in the three-point position. Then the tail came up and the ship came off the ground.

"Gear up," Sutton commanded.

Griffin toggled the switch and the wheels retracted smoothly. He checked the gauges. The engine's sound droned and vibrated the fuselage as the ground dropped away.

Rowe wondered if he'd live through the required missions. He didn't look through the nose canopy; it would only compound his fear and his deep dislike for the airplane and the men flying her—especially the haughty Griffin, with his wealth displayed arrogantly in his shimmering blue eyes.

The Chief remained deeply suspicious: he was working on a plan to discover the history of *The Beast*, something that would reveal her spirit.

But Bush could only think of himself and his purpose. His thoughts weren't on teamwork or the other crewmen; he thought about his reason for being here, which was separate and apart from the other crewmen.

As *The Beast* ascended, Baker barely felt the nose nudging upward. He'd been through this dozens of times and the tap of the engines was something distant, something that occasionally distracted his attention from the novel he was reading.

Kid Kiley wondered how many more missions he could complete before Wing administration finished their investigation concerning his age.

Tutone, self-proclaimed war lover, took a deep breath and filled his lungs. Combat was the only thing that mattered. Combat was a world of deadly excitement, an atmosphere of paradox and mystery. He was a man split by two emotions: his head told him combat could be fatal, and yet there was a compulsion to engage the monster of fear, to embrace it and kiss its cruel lips, to smell it, to taste it and see it, to come as close to it as possible without dying. He wondered if the others ever felt the same.

The only thing that drew these men together was a sheet of paper that contained their names. Chance drew them into the air, nothing else. Although they flew together, each was taken up with his own fear.

That afternoon *The Beast* flew up and down the English coast; then easterly and back again toward the Channel. She was coaxed and prodded, pampered and kicked. But all within the prescribed limits of AN 01-20EF-1—*The Pilot's Flight Operating Instructions for Army Models B-17F and G.* Her flaps were not lowered at speeds in excess of 147 MPH; she was not driven earthward beyond 270 MPH; her manifold pressure never exceeded forty six inches. She wasn't put into a spin, rolled, looped, or flown inverted (although Griffin, in a moment of characteristic boast, said that he could do a loop).

Sutton and Griffin took turns landing and taking off, flying at the varied power settings. Sutton was beginning to hate Griffin. His baby face and blond hair were reflected in the windscreen, and each time Sutton looked up he saw the two men with their double-breasted suits asking him to test fly the *Aerohound* so Roger wouldn't injure a toenail days later before a crowd of thousands. Each time he performed a manuever he'd say to Sutton and Tutone, "Easy. Piece of cake," until Sutton told him to shut up and fly.

Sutton would call out a procedure for Griffin and Griffin would perform it with textbook precision. This annoyed Sutton, because he wanted to see Griffin fail. No one that self-centered deserved everything. Sutton had to work for everything he had: money, flying, everything. And he did it silently, without boasting. Tutone sensed the tension between them.

"Stop the number two engine," Sutton called out, wondering if world-famous aviator knew the proper procedure.

Griffin moved the mixture control to

"engine off," stopped the booster pump, and pressed the feathering switch. He didn't hesitate. Sutton turned the ignition switch to "engine off" when the prop jerked still and Griffin immediately closed the cowl flaps. The throttle was shut down and the trim tabs were adjusted for the change in flight character.

"Well, now what?" Sutton asked Griffin.

The answer came quickly. "Now the automatic flight control switches are turned on."

"What happens when the number two engine is shut down?" Sutton asked, staring at Griffin.

He hesitated, then said, "The vacuum pump is inoperative and you have to set the selector valve to another pump."

"And the de-icer pressure? What happens to that?"

No answer. Griffin's peach skin turned bright red.

Sutton said, "You think this is like flying one of those fancy puddle-hoppers back home, don't you? Well, it ain't. It takes more than a fancy flying scarf and a lot of trophies to fly this bitch and you'd better learn it fast. Now, when the vacuum pump is inoperative the de-icer pressure is reduced and the de-icer vacuum will not be available. The de-icer systems will therefore operate inefficiently. Just like you. You better learn that, and it better be soon."

Tutone knew that the boy aviator wasn't so hot after all, that he couldn't compare with Jim Sutton.

That night at the Officers' Club, Sutton was sitting with Griffin and the spunky T.R. Reed.

What Griffin possessed in the way of over-confidence and nonchalance, so did the beautiful T.R. At twenty three, the Nevada lieutenant with the nice breasts and striking features knew that she was a beauty. She knew that few females were flying the famous B-17 and the hot P-38 *Lightning*, and she told anyone who'd listen just how deft she was.

"Emergencies," she said. "I'm really cool in an emergency. I guess I've always been a clear, fast thinker. A month ago, coming out of Baker's Field, I lost the number two fan on a '38, but I had the manual memorized for such an emergency."

Sutton rolled his brown eyes.

"What happened?" the beaming Griffin asked, living the moment with her, certain he'd be impressed.

"First thing," she said, "I got some altitude real fast, then cut the gun on the dead engine."

"Then," Griffin interrupted, "you probably adjusted the trim and—"

"Hey!" T.R. said, "Who's milking this

cow! You astonish me, Rog, you really and truly do."

Sutton said. "But T.R., you are talking to the man who's flown the dreaded outside loop. Please show a little respect."

"Respect, crap," T.R. answered. "This boy"—she patted his head—"practiced that a dozen times and led the world to believe that was his first show, I know it."

Sutton smiled. "Wanna bet? I never lose a bet."

"Anyway," T.R. said, "I got the fan feathered and got more height and brought the bird back over the field upside down on the one good engine." She inverted her hand over the beer bottle strewn table. "Just to show the old folks at the factory that it didn't matter how badly they slapped a '38 together, that it would take more than that to squash ol' T.R."

"You landed safely, I trust," Griffin said.

"You trust? Gee, does a duck swim?"

"Only," Sutton said, grinning, "if his asshole's watertight." T.R. and Griffin looked at him and laughed. "And," Sutton added. "I betcha yours is sewn together tight as a drum."

"You bet your wings, bus driver. And goophers and eggs," she said, referring to first class aviators and novices, "have tried to tap it but nobody's come close." She punched the air with a petite fist.

Her smile, the bright spark of her teeth,

the full lips and wavy hair falling over square shoulders, the shape of her slim eyebrows and high cheekbones, reminded Sutton of Rita Hayworth. In his mind he undressed her: the buttons unraveled on her crisp Army blouse and her breasts spilled out. The pink nipples were hard with excitement. Her skirt slipped off and her panties skidded down her lean legs. Her body hair was perfectly shaped, a triangle. She held her sex open and offered it, looking pained but pleased. At the last second, he refused her.

Now, she smiled and he smiled back. Maybe, he thought, she was thinking the same thing. He winked at her and hoped Griffin saw it. T.R. winked back with equal deliberance.

Later that evening, Griffin asked Colonel Parker if he could borrow his room — "So I can take care of that ferry pilot over there with the big knockers." When he heard the request, Parker felt a twinge of envy and readily consented to the well-known flyer.

Most officers slept in a hall-shaped building with provisions for only one or two private rooms. Acquisition of the rooms had nothing to do with rank, but longevity. As each pilot left (or was killed) the others would move up one bunk until they moved into a private room. It wasn't uncommon for a room to be borrowed for an evening. That night, Parker had plans with an Army nurse, "a friend," he said. The nurse, having tired of Air Force surroundings, had somehow acquired an English flat in the village and would, in Parker's words, "be creating a delightful ambience of house keeping for the next several days." Since he'd be gone that evening, Griffin and T.R. would have a place to "talk about the war in greater depth," which was Griffin's line to the shrewd female avaitor.

Griffin had eight bottles of beer, while the calculating T.R. had nursed herself through a meager three, somehow eschewing the boy aviator's plan for getting her fully skunked. Roger, beery-brained and primed for a quick kill felt assured that his prey was ready to give in to his charm.

Their laughter and whispered words traced their path as they made their way through the darkness between the Officers' Club and Parker's room. As they went, the sweet brassy notes of the club orchestra followed them.

Griffin locked the door and plopped on the edge of Parker's neat bed. He took off his shoes and popped the tops off two bottles of Pabst beer.

"It's stuffy in here," T.R. said, opening the window.

"Come over here and let's talk."

"Sure."

She sat on the foot of the bed, tossing her hair back over her shoulders.

One dim desk lamp washed the plain furniture and dull green walls. T.R. said, "What do you want to talk about, Rog?"

"Nothin'," he slurred.

"I didn't think so. But listen," she said, unbuttoning the top button of her tunic, "I understand that Parker has you and the crew pegged for a big deal classified mission. That's why he had Jim Sutton transferred."

Roger raised his eyebrows. "Yeah. I heard that, too. Anyway, I don't want to talk about that now." His ice-blue eyes were glazed, like balls of ice.

"I didn't think so. Well, then what would you like to do?" she asked, getting up and walking to the desk.

Griffin snapped his head back, gulped some beer, and laughed.

"What do you think?"

T.R. unbuttoned her woolen jacket and freed the weight of her breasts. She stubbed out her cigarette and grabbed a small brassy object from the desk. "I don't think Jim likes you, Roger."

Roger patted the foot of the bed. "Come here."

"Look, why don't we do this right?" she said, and walked over to Roger. "Take off your clothes, and I'll take off mine, and we'll talk about whatever's on your mind. How's that sound?"

"Excellent. Very excellent." He stood and placed the beer on the night table and began to undress. "Sutton doesn't like me 'cause he's jealous."

"I don't think that's it, Roger."

From the Officers' Club, a song the orchestra was playing wafted into the room. The vocalist had begun to sing the popular Harold Arlen-Johnny Mercer composition, *Blues In The Night*.

> *My momma done told me, when I was*
> *in pigtails*
> *A man will sweet talk you and give*
> *you the eye*
> *But when the talkin's done, a man's a*
> *two-faced*
> *Worrisome thing who'll lead you to*
> *sing*
> *The blues in the night*

"My God," T.R. whispered, "you do have a magnificent body."

"Yes, well, I mean, I know. I've been thinking about yours ever since I saw you pop outta the ship."

"How romantic," T.R. said, giggling.

Roger stood, dropped his trousers. Only his olive-drab boxer shorts remained.

"How 'bout you," he said. "Why don'cha lemme help you with your shirt or somethin'."

"You know something, Roger, you're a handsome man," T.R. said, with her best sultry voice. "You really know how to get a woman . . . aroused. If you know what I mean."

"Sure do."

She gave his ear lobe a little nibble.

The evening breeze will start the trees
to crying
The blues in the night
And the moon will hide its light
When you get the blues in the night
And take my word
That mockingbird
Will sing the saddest song
He knows things are wrong
And he's so right

Roger brought a booze-heavy arm around T.R.'s shoulder and leaned in for a peck.

"Listen," T.R. said, pulling her head away, "women are a little different than men. A woman has to . . . to get . . . wet."

The word hit Roger with erotic force. "Are you . . . wet?"

"Not yet. That's why we have to take our time — to give me time to get ready for you."

"Oh Jesus, yes!" Roger fell back on the bed, assured now that he was on the right beam, that within minutes ol' T.R. would be *soaking*, ready for him. He never missed, he thought. How could he? Good looks. Charm. Reputation. The family name. He never missed.

"Now, sweetheart, I'm going to undress

for you." She smiled. "I'm going to turn the light out first."

Roger propped himself on his elbow. *"No!* No, don't I want . . . I want to . . . watch."

"I can't dear. I get embarrassed."

He waved his hand and fell back on the bed, anticipating, giving in to compromise, waiting to sense her warm body next to his.

From Natchez to Mobile
From Mobile to Saint Joe
Where the four winds, they might
blow
I've been in some big towns
And I've heard me some big talk
But there is one thing I know

T.R. turned off the light and walked gently to the pot-bellied stove in the center of the room. The stove shone orange in the dark; the coals were fresh and hot. Quietly, she opened the stove's door and dropped the brass object into the coals.

"Do you know," she asked, "what a Very pistol is?"

"Yes."

"What is it?"

"It's a flare gun that we use to signal wounded or dead aboard a B-17. What . . . what do you care . . . ?"

"Because," she said, tiptoeing toward the opened window, "just before I turned the light out you looked like you had a Very pistol in your undies."

Griffin laughed. "I do. And it's going to go off real soon."

"It sure is."

T.R.'s strong young legs pulled her through the window easily, quietly. With her feet planted on the lawn outside the window and her head stuck through, she said:

"Roger, honey. I'm undressed now. Why don't you just rest there like that and slip off your underpants, and I'll come over and . . . you know what."

Without getting up, Roger slipped off his underpants and tossed them through the dark room. He was fully primed; his eyes were closed, filled with visions of a naked T.R.

In a willowy tone, T.R. said, "I'm all wet for you now."

When the Very shell exploded in the stove it filled the room with a bright orange fury. T.R. ducked. The room blossomed with exploding soot and covered Roger's running, naked figure as it flashed toward the door.

The last vision T.R. had, as she wiped the tears of laughter from her face, was a blackened Roger disappearing into the evening.

CHAPTER SEVEN

Sutton's new outfit, the 45th Bombardment Group, had a raid the next day to the airport at Liege, Belgium. Gossip was that it would be one of those sweet milk runs, a chance to rack up another mission and come home to steak and onions.

Sutton was asleep at 0400 hours when Sergeant Litton came around banging beds and stabbing their eyes with the beam from his powerful flashlight.

"Rise and shine, breakfast in half an hour. Briefing at 0515. Rise and shine."

Litton had a voice made from old tree bark and rusty steel. Everyone was certain that's why they picked him. It would've been easier waking to a pistol or cannon shot. He went about his task with cheer, smacking the cots, cluncking along the wooden flooring with oversized boots that banged like hammers. His wake-up times varied, depending on weather conditions, the mission; but everyone anticipated him by several seconds—it was the distinct scuff of his feet that announced his arrival. When Litton arrived, a mission arrived; when Litton was absent, a mission did not exist.

While the pilots were emerging from deep sleep, Sutton remained tucked in. He felt guilty. At 0401 he checked the glow of his watch and remembered the nightmare.

He was piloting the lead ship, which was nameless, and below him and to the rear were three B-17s: *Naughty Nancy, Sweet Sue,* and *Spot Remover.* They were somewhere over France. They were at 19,000 feet and the sky was a pilot's sky: clear, limitless, tranquil. Behind them swirled clouds of vapor trails, which spilled from their engines like smoky chalk. Sutton knew the pilots of each ship, and that made the dream much worse, more real: Breton, *Naughty Nancy's* commander; Farley, at twenty the youngest pilot in the Group, and the commander of *Sweet Sue;* and *Spot Remover's* pilot, Chuck Chase. The Fortresses glided through the air, soundless brown and green flying insects against the blue heavens above a pale green planet. They seemed to have no purpose today. Sutton felt powerless. Two Fw-190s appeared; no one announced their arrival. They were stunning, with their blunt noses and pale-blue underbellies. They spiraled and swept, rolled and dove, flattened and turned. Graceful. Lazy. Fast. Propellers caught the sun and shone like crystal. The wings were delicate, crisp against the sky. Sometimes their forms turned black and they silhouetted against the sun's gold light. Canopies sparkled like gemstones. Their pilots pranced them around, appearing to show off, hot-rodding before they chewed up the B-17s.

Suddenly they took their fighters into a neat power-off climb and they momentarily hung on their props. They winged over and dove, and Sutton could hear the sharp crack of the BMW radial engines catching when the power came back on. They circled and made a head-on sweep into the formation. Sutton saw them clearly. The rudders were yellow with red trim tabs. The *spiral-schnauze*—the prop's spinner—was spiraled black and white. One fighter had a large number "13" on its fuselage, the other a "5"; both numbers were in front of the *Balkenkruz*. Sutton heard them streak overhead and wondered why the gunners hadn't fired. He shouted over the interphone; no one replied. He was outraged and wanted to choke the gunners and fire the guns himself. He made his way through each gun position but the triggers wouldn't work. Nothing happened. Not a bullet was fired. *"They're going to kill us!"* No one replied.

The Germans appeared again, coming from the eleven o'clock position in line-abreast formation. They were A-2 models with bulged access panels in the wings for the synchronized 20mm Mauser 151 and FF cannons. The engines were improved BMW 801C-2s, which required less maintenance time than the earlier models used during the Battle of Britain. Within a range of 300 yards the cannons sparkled. Sutton put a gloved hand in front of his eyes but the vision did not disappear. Spent shell casings rained black from the wing chutes. Black gunsmoke trailed behind. Someone screamed. Sutton didn't know who. *Naughty Nancy* erupted, and pieces of her body floated like crazy metal wafers. *Spot Remover* flamed and nosed over and made a straight line toward the earth. She vanished in a sheet of orange flame. Sutton heard the thump. The port wing of *Sweet Sue* broke off like a bread stick and the wing root flared into a sheet of white gas-flame. Three seconds later there was a shattering explosion in the bomb bay. It sent a shock wave rippling through the sky, and the ship fell in three large smoky pieces. There were no parachutes from any of the planes. The Germans appeared again, sweeping around on their port wings, 13 high, 5 low, taking their time for the killing blow. Sutton tried to work the controls of his bomber, but like the machine guns, he got no response. The enemy performed a split-S, and when they returned they came toward the starboard wing in a step formation. The Mauser cannons flashed and then there was a blinding white light.

"Captain Sutton, sir," said Litton. "Time to rise and shine, sir."

"Get that damned light out of my eyes."

"Are you flying today, sir?"

"Got a training mission. What's the weather?"

"Spotty. There might be a delay."

Sutton threw the covers off and looked at his watch again—0402. He moved down to his footlocker for his cigarettes and lit one.

Capt. Richard Page, who slept in the cot next to Sutton's, had slipped into his G.I. underwear and was working his way into a flight suit. He was meticulous and had his gear laid out the night before, planned, so there would be no missing part of his flying outfit. Quietly, he called out each item as he slipped it on, stepped into it, snapped it, or buckled it. After his flying boots he called out his cigarettes, the last item. Same thing in his aircraft—everything was done with a number. Someone asked him if he made love that way and he'd said, "Yes. So I know what comes first and what comes last."

Sutton leaned on his cot. "They got me assigned to a special mission with an odd-ball crew."

"Yeah," Page said. "The word got around fast."

"People say it's just a glory chase for Parker and he doesn't really care if we come back or not—it's the effort that'll make him look good."

"I heard that, too."

In the distance a dog barked. There were muffled voices, the rustle of boots on the pathway, the soft idle of a jeep's engine.

Page shifted his weight and his leather flying jacket creaked. Sutton opened one eye, to make sure his friend was still there. Page coughed. He was getting itchy. He said, "Whatever it is they picked for you to do, they picked the right man."

They shook hands and Sutton said, "Good luck today, Dick."

"Yeah—luck and skill. That's all it is."

After the briefing the crews converged on waiting, warmed bombers. Mechanics were standing around, hands in coveralls, watching the parade of trucks. They'd been at it all night, tweaking the engines, the hydraulics, whatever needed to be wiped, filled, plugged, patched, beaten, bolted, or bent. Now they were resigned—it was the crew's turn to bitch after takeoff that a screw was loose, an instrument didn't read correctly, or a cowling didn't open or close—a recurring problem on the B-17.

From a hilly lawn dotted with red and white poppies a short distance off, Tutone and Sutton were spectators to a familiar procession. They felt like outcasts, children watching their classmates leaving for school without them. Tutone picked one and sniffed it. "A milk-run," he said, watching the crews lugging their gear off idling trucks.

Tutone and Sutton sensed excitement out there—the manner in which the men moved their bodies, their gestures, their postures. If it were another mission, something predictably serious, they'd be moving with the agility of musclebound weightlifters—serious, stoic, quiet. Not this morning. Liege is to be a milk-run, and that's what today is about.

Tutone chucked a poppy through the air and watched it arc and tumble on the lawn; the petals exploded white. He said, "Do you know that there are guys down there who'd give both nuts to be standing up here with us instead of going off on another mission? I would take anybody's place. Any one of them." He bent over and plucked another flower and began to rip the petals away from the short stem.

Without looking at Tutone, Sutton said: "Why do you like it so much?"

"Because—" Tutone picked another poppy. "What are you asking me for, boss? You're a pilot, you know. You love it, too."

"I like it, yeah, but I don't like getting my ass shot at."

"But that's part of it. That's a part you like, too, but you just won't admit it like me. Me, I don't care. I mean, I don't mind it. Can you believe that?"

"You're nuts, Benny Tutone, you really are."

"No, I ain't."

Sutton shook his head.

"Look," Tutone said, "it's a game. It's like hunting. There's a special thrill about it—about who can outfox who."

"And what about the possibility that a German will outfox you and blow that big head off in that damned turret of yours?"

"Naw," said Tutone, almost singing the word. "It don't affect me. I don't give a shit about that." He was watching the crews standing around the planes. "And you know what else, boss? I think you love it just as much as me. I look at it this way: They give us a 17 and they let us borrow it for a while. The airplane costs, what, a hundred and eighty or a hundred and ninety thousand bucks? Anyway, look at them ships." He pointed a finger at the *Mairzy Doats*, Dick Page's plane. "You can feel the power from here, the destructive force. All's that plane is is a bomb holder, that's what she is. A container for a load of dynamite wrapped in a tube with four Wright engines bolted on her beautiful body. Then they tell us where to go, where to drop that sweet load—just like you tell a cab driver, 'Here, drop me off here.' And we go there and we drop that sweet load, and we come back—"

"*Maybe* you come back."

"*Maybe?* Horseshit maybe. Benny Tutone

and Jim Sutton always come back. We're invincible. That's what we shoulda called our new ship—*The Invincible.*"

"You're nuts," Sutton said, with his lopsided grin.

"Nah." Tutone gave a laugh, a devilish sound. He brought the poppy up and took another long, deep whiff, then stuck the stem into his mouth. He continued: "If this was any simpler it would be boring—like wearing a blue uniform and flying wealthy jerks between New York and Miami Beach. That's not for me, boss, and it ain't for you, either," he said, checking the shine on his boots.

"I suppose not, but it is a clean way to make a buck," Sutton said, thinking about his father's airfield and what they might do after the war was over.

Tutone brushed a speck of grass off his boot and said: "War lets you find out who you are real fast."

"Then you must like affairs with hot ladies."

"War is the ultimate thrill," Tutone said. "That's what I call it." He spit the poppy from his mouth.

"I call it murder."

At 0735 Sutton checked his watch.

Sunlight shimmered the tarmac and lit the trees. Low ground haze had burned off.

Some of the B-17s, the unpainted silver models, shone like polished flatware from where Sutton and Tutone stood.

The entire Group had been prepared for Liege, and Col. Branch Parker was delighted, knowing that every ship available would be in the air. He was in his jeep approaching the dispersal area, like a football coach about to prime the team before the big game.

"You've got to have that burning desire," was the remark he used continually.

Now he was mingling with the crews, goosing them up with his burning desire jive before they took off on their raid. He instructed his driver, Sergeant Cole, to move down the rows of poised Fortresses — past *Naughty Nancy* and *The City of Chicago*. He waved as he went. When he came to *Erotic Neurotic* he threw his head back and struck his arms out to the heavens asking for mock forgiveness for the art work displayed on the nose section.

Erotic Neurotic had a detailed drawing of a naked woman sitting on a blanket on a small patch of grass. Her long lithe legs were spread, but angled away from the viewer, revealing just a spot of divine, golden pubic hair. The face was girlishly seductive, the lips puckered, tempting everyone to kiss her. Her long flowing hair cascaded over her slender back; her stomach was flat, her waist trim and tightly drawn in. She dazzled every male that looked at her, even the tight-assed Parker who couldn't resist a longer than usual stare. She had what was generally accepted in the Group as the "most perfect set of tits on the face of the earth."

It was ritual for the crew to climb up a ladder held by the chief mechanic and plant a gentle smooch on the erect, pink-tipped right nipple prior to every mission. They did this with their eyes closed, with relish. It was for this psychological reason that Irontail Parker, smiling as he drove by, allowed the milk-skinned lady with the pilot's cap and nothing else, to remain emblazoned on the side of one of America's fighting ships. The crew waved back with perfunct smiles.

Parker continued past *Wona Mona, Hazey, My Gosh!, Pucker Up,* and *Say It Isn't So,* which had a few bars of the Irving Berlin song written out below the title.

When he reached *Firepower, Inc.* and the *Chattanooga Chew-Chew,* he had the jeep slip in between the planes and jumped out with athletic grace. He slapped a few butts, doing the football coach routine to perfection.

Tutone and Sutton watched in silence.

Sutton cocked his head back and looked up.

"It's a good sky," he said.

Tutone grunted agreement. "How 'bout goin' to town after our training run?"

"Swell."

Parker was almost through. When he reached *Patch O' Pleasure* he stood in the jeep and faked a few jabs and punches for the crew—the go-give-'em-hell gesture—then blew a kiss to the drawing on the nose section: a naked woman holding a slim white towel that dangled over the object of the ship's name. He went on, calling out to the crew of *Moonlight Moanin'*, *The New York Clipper*, *Sweet Sue*, *Spot Remover*, *Prissy Missy*, *Air Hound*, and *#10 Bus*.

Parker was one of those officers who was very aware of his personal image and what effect it might have on anyone around him—how it would influence or persuade them toward his goals. He wanted to make brigadier general before his fortieth birthday. He was a West Point grad, a square-shouldered ramrod-straight man that seemed to step from the pages of a society magazine, replete with custom-made uniforms, blue eyes, and suntanned skin. His gift of bullshit was known through the Air Force. He'd moved through the officers' ranks with speed and agility, flashing the West Point ring on anyone of higher rank who might be provincial enough not to recognize the cut of the aviator standing before him. He had the gift of persuasion, the ability to perceive people of importance who, ultimately, could be used to further his Air Force career. The jeep stopped near the crew of *This Is It!*, commanded by the most disliked command pilot in the Group, Capt. Archer R. Chrisp.

Chrisp and Parker hit it off like milk and cookies. Although there was an eighteen-year age difference, Chrisp's youth did nothing to defer the solidity between the two men; and the fact that Chrisp was also a West Point grad did nothing but add to the relationship. The Chrisp family was important to Parker. Chrisp's father was a major general stationed in the new Pentagon building, and he was on the board of officers who passed decisions on the elevation of colonels to the rank of brigadier general.

Egocentric, lofty, Chrisp was often used by Parker as an example of the American bomber pilot for visiting press and celebrities. Each of Chrisp's crewmen wore a specially tailored silk scarf cut from the parachute of what they called "an outstanding German fighter ace" that their tail-gunner, Joe Jones, had supposedly bagged over the Channel. The German pilot was supposed to have died in captivity five days later. Chrisp and the crew got the parachute, the German's collar insignia, his Walther PPK pistol, his boots, cuff title, and special *Luftwaffe* officer's belt buckle. They had everything but the pilot's underwear, they said, and swore vengeance on the English seamen who said the pilot was not wearing his Knight's Cross. Colonel Parker had given them permission to fly up north, to Great Yarmouth, to collect their booty.

Chrisp was often photographed smiling for magazines and newspapers, his face turned toward the clouds, his B-17 poised for action in the background. Naming the ship *This Is It!* wasn't a random decision. Parker loved it. When Parker hitched a ride with a crew, or suggested a plane to a visiting newsman, the task automatically went to Chrisp's aircraft. Eventually, Chrisp started to become a celebrity, to mingle with the best knives and forks in England. What really bothered the rest of the crews was that Chrisp was bedding down with some of England's finest birds.

Parker talked with the Chrisp crew now; they circled him like a team eager to hear the coach. They were silent, pensive, as they listened to the pedantic colonel give them a pep talk. Parker of course did not announce that he would be monitoring the Liege raid from the safety of Group Headquarters with Rag Tag asleep at his feet. There was a moment of prayerful silence, and then Parker moved smoothly back into his jeep.

At 0750 everyone who had to take a last-minute pee before zipping up ran for the bushes. Rag Tag scampered behind gleefully and found a sapling and raised his leg.

Sutton and Tutone were sitting on the lawn, chewing blades of grass, waiting for the takeoff. They'd only viewed the process once, when they first arrived at Bassingbourn; and now they felt they were looking at the war through the wrong end of the periscope. A few moments ago Sergeant Holden had pulled up in a jeep and told them the training mission was postponed because of a faulty fuel pump in their new ship.

Colonel Parker had been ordered to send up two squadrons against Liege: the 367th Fightin' Hellcats, and the 368th Jolly Rogers, Sutton's new squadron assignment within the Group. The other two squadrons—the 369th and 444th—were ordered to stand down for a possible afternoon raid on Fe Camp, France. Once he received the go-ahead from Wing, Parker had secured the best seat in the house for the impressive takeoff procession—he was near the runway, the spot where the bombers lifted off, and was prepared to give twenty planes the thumbs-up sign and a crisp salute. The jittery Rag Tag, sensing the energy of the takeoff, was seated in the back of the jeep, his tail flogging the cushion.

The *Fightin' Hellcats* were commanded by Sutton's friend, Capt. Richard Page, the command pilot of *Mairzy Doats*. Sutton respected Page, trusted him. The 29-year-old Page was a career Air Force officer and knew airplanes. He was gentle, soft spoken, and rarely barked out an order: he led by example.

The number one engine of *Doats* cracked

the morning calm. Amber light caught her spinning props as each engine fired.

There were ten aircraft in each squadron and the ground trembled, shook, under the roar of their 1,200-horsepower engines.

The scent of fresh grass vanished. The air filled with the strong odor of engine exhaust.

Parker was up on the hood of the jeep, hands on hips, waiting for the first B-17 to make the turn from the taxiway onto the runway.

Now the bombers came off their hardstands. Page turned the *Doats* onto the runway then gave the ship full throttle. His boots came off the brakes and the engines sucked air, roared, and the propellers blurred silver.

A small crowd on the far side of the runway made a cheering motion but the sound was lost in the plane's drone.

The aircraft hesitated then rolled and began to speed down the runway, a slim arrow streaking against a framework of green countryside. When the wheels appeared to leave the concrete, the crowd made a cheering motion.

A hat flew into the air, a pair of gloves followed. Parker did his routine: thumbs-up, a salute.

Then something wrong happened.

Sutton and Tutone saw it.

"Shit!"

"What the hell . . . ?"

Mairzy Doats seemed burdened. Overweight and underpowered.

"It don't sound right!" shouted Tutone over the roar. He grabbed Sutton's arm.

The bomber was halfway down the runway and both of them could tell from the engine sound and the altitude that something was cockeyed. She should've been higher and farther down the runway.

"Get it down on the ground!" Tutone yelled, waving his arms. "Not enough power! Not enough power!"

Page had one and a half seconds to decide between getting airborne or slapping the plane back down on the runway.

Sutton motioned with his arms to put it down.

Four streaks of bluish-gray smoke plumed from the exhaust stacks.

Parker was on the jeep's hood preparing to wave to *Erotic Neurotic;* her engines were chugging as she waited her turn. Rag Tag was panting nervously on the driver's seat.

Mairzy Doats continued lugging through the air. The engines tapped out sour notes. They sounded sick. One of them coughed, gagged, seemed to mechanically vomit. The nose came up slightly, wanted to get airborne, to get normal. The words *Mairzy Doats* were visible, along with the little lamb climbing the string of ivy.

In the cockpit, Page and his copilot couldn't trace the problem — there just wasn't enough power coming off the fans to bring the lumbering bitch off the concrete.

At one hundred feet, *Doats* was in a position of indecision—an awful place for a pilot at a moment like this. Page had apparently changed his mind and was thinking of landing.

"More power!" the copilot roared.

"It's on full for God's sakes!"

The tail gunner sensed something horrible was about to happen. There was a little spot on his ass, a certain sensitive point that told him when things weren't working. On the runway, there was an oil smear, and according to his primitive but accurate calculations, the whole enchilada, as he called the plane, was supposed to be higher and more distant after it passed this stain. He listened. The engines were skipping and the runway was ending. "Oh Jesus," he muttered to himself. Impulsively, he reached back for the emergency latch on the small door to his compartment.

But it was too late. Beyond the runway there was a small field surrounded by a knee-high stone fence, and a tree line that was broken by a caretaker's shed. It was the only choice left.

"Jesus God," said Page, his face lighting with horror. He knew.

He was hunched over the control column wrestling with the ailerons, the rudder pedals, trying to work miracles with them.

He wanted to get the bird off the ground. But he made up his mind too late.

Sutton knew. Parker knew. Tutone knew. Even Rag Tag sensed something odd. Everyone. They all knew.

"Page was a good man," Sutton said softly, watching *Mairzy Doats* skimming the treetops. A few leaves fluttered to the ground.

"Oh no," Tutone mumbled.

Page knew an instant before it happened.

The props trimmed the trees like big scythes, palsied, spun like eleven-foot-wide Dutch windmills caught by a wispy breeze. The noise stopped. The ship was a powerless arrow, a smear of hopelessness fading across bright blue sky. The wings fluttered and disappeared beyond the trees in the distance.

Page knew an instant before it happened.

He tried to flatten her, to lift her away, to steer her tonnage with his whole body, his power and intelligence, into the stars, into the heaven where she belonged, to handle her like the good pilot he was. But she resisted him, failed to obey the commands of his hands, refused his desire, his wish for life for himself and his crew.

Her engines died, and her tail went down and smacked the craggy field. That's when Richard Page was certain that he had scragged it forever. "Jesus God, oh no . . ."

The *Doats* had taken the dive.

Four thousand pounds of American HE bombs did what they'd been designed to do—all of them. The shock wave snapped trees and picked up rock, lifted 30-foot-high steel hangar doors off ball-bearing rollers and slapped them to the ground. A large portion of stone fencing vanished. People in a car a quarter-mile away were pelted and cut by splintered glass and flying debris. Rag Tag jerked off the jeep, howling, as if stung by a bee. Parker was almost blown off the hood. Windows in buildings adjacent to the end of the runway were snowed. In the fifty-foot hole of exposed English soil, shreds of metal and engine chunks and insulation rested smoldering. Wing spars, wiring, tubing—everything was melted, burned, and baked in the explosive flash. Grass in a hundred-yard radius was singed black.

Sutton was speechless. A tear burned his cheek.

CHAPTER EIGHT

At noon, after Dick Page died, Sutton and Tutone were half-drunk at the Rainbow Corner, a converted Lyons restaurant at the corner of Shaftesbury Avenue and Windmill Street, a big G.I. club where Hollywood sent its stars and America its young soldiers.

The place was jumping. There was a band beating out a boogie and Tutone kept time, swacking the table with a pencil, watching the cookies flying around the floor. He was so horny he felt pained.

"It's right here," he said, holding his crotch and heart. "Not here." He slapped his forehead. "I never use that for anything."

"I know, I know," said Sutton.

A young woman with mounds of blonde hair came sweeping past; she glanced at Tutone and kept going, then a second later she swept back and stopped. "Any gum, chum?" she asked.

Tutone wiggled his eyebrows and reached

into his pocket and pulled out a pack of Wrigley's, still sealed, *virgo intacto*. A confectionery jewel.

The woman's face lit up; she smiled and showed a wall of white teeth.

"Here," Tutone said. "Chew the whole pack but take the wrapper off first. Only stipulation is, I gotta watch."

She laughed and threw her silky hair back and ripped the seal off the wrapper and sat down. In a moment she was in gum heaven, chewing the stuff like a novice. "This is ambrosia," she said.

"Jesus," Tutone shouted above the band, "I'm talkin' to an angel!"

"I think I'm leaving," Sutton said.

"Hey, wait! You can't leave," Tutone said. "This young lady is going to take herself and her gum to the stars. You should stay here and watch, boss."

Sutton left.

Tutone watched the woman's jaw manipulating the first stick. "The best piece," he said, "is the one you have just before bed time."

She smiled.

They took a taxi to her place. She took the third stick of gum (the second was undressed in the rear of the taxi) and unfolded the foil with the same precision she would use to unravel his zipper. Slowly, she tongued the underside, feeling the weight. Then she dabbled on the top and stained the confectionery sugar. She sucked half of it into her mouth.

Tutone asked: "What goes in hard and comes out soft?"

He had her panties around her ankles and was lingering on her calves, kissing her sugar-coated lips.

"Gum and you," she finally answered after a few seconds of thought.

"No."

She looked surprised, certain she had the answer.

"What then, love?" she asked.

"Pasta."

"*Pasta?*"

"Yeah, pasta. You know—just before you stick it in the boiling water it's good and hard, and when you slip it out its very soft."

"I like gum and you better."

"So do I."

His hand moved across her thick pubic bush. She carefully took the gum from her mouth and placed it on the foil on the night table and turned the light off. She took his head into her hands and looked into his black eyes and she said: "Tell me what you like. Tell me what drives you crazy."

Her blouse was off and he took her bra and tossed it into the half-light and continued brushing her satiny cheeks with his lips.

"You," he said, "drive me crazy." She was stroking him slowly. Flower-soft motions.

While she worked her hand there he thought of Page and the *Doats* slicing through the treetops. And then he felt guilty, resting there beside the woman. But if he stopped her, would Page come back? Would it matter? Of course not. But he still felt bad, then quickly put it aside.

She was up naked now and went over the edge of the bed and had her small firm shoulders flat against the thick-piled rug, showing him that she was athletic and supple, that she could maneuver with agility and grace, that she was a little kinky. Her short muscular legs were over the bed's edge, knees parted, buttocks resting there, waiting for him.

"Do you like this? Does this drive you nutty?" she whispered. She was holding herself open with the fingers of one hand, titillating herself with the finger of the other.

He took her with his lips and tongue, and her hips jerked as if sparked by a strong bolt of electricity. While she quivered, she held his head with strong hands.

This excited him the way combat did. The glory of both, the sound of the guns jerking in his turret, the scent of cordite stinging his nostrils the way her taste did. Page was gone. Now he thought about this and combat. About himself and what he was doing here, and the two were equal, flashing through his mind. He couldn't wait until he did them both again because he loved them, absolutely loved them. Combat and sex.

She gasped, slurred her words, rolled her eyes, and she flailed her head as she went further and further. She was a swimmer and her swimmer's arms pushed him away and she heeled around on her firm buttocks and opened herself on the bed and guided him in. Her first orgasm shocked him and the second surprised him because of the explosive force. Then it was over and she rested, perspiring, holding him.

"I could use a sip," she said.

"Water?"

She nodded.

He got up and brought back a large crystal glass filled with water she took it and mumbled for more. She said she'd been at Bassingbourn twice and really admired the Yanks and what they were doing, and that she wanted to see him again. He said yes.

"What do you do?" she asked.

"I'm a gunner—a turret gunner and a flight engineer in a B-17."

"Do you want more?"

"Water?"

"No, silly." She giggled.

"Oh—yes, in a while."

She laughed easily, that was her way, and then kissed his forehead and sat up. He took the gum from the foil and gave it to her, placed it in her mouth.

"Sugar is energy," he said. He stroked her tight stomach.

She said: "I swim a lot. That's why I'm so tight. I'd like to go to the Olympics when this whole bloody war is over."

"Yeah. I can feel it." He ran his hand through her body hair again. She got up and went to his leather jacket and took out his smokes, lit one for both of them and settled alongside him like a cat.

"Are you afraid—I mean, aren't you scared of dying, of getting shot down?" she asked.

"Nah. Never think about it." He blew smoke to the ceiling. "You see, you can't go up with that attitude. You think about it sometimes but you don't let it linger for long. You can't meditate on it."

"I admire you. For what you do—what you're doing for England."

"I do it for me, don't kid yourself. I do it because I love it." He felt proud. "I never had anything else in my life and now I have something. I've got a part in a war, and I'm not afraid. I'm part of something."

"History?"

"Yeah. History. We are the most destructive men in the history of mankind. We destroy and that is our work, and I love it." His fingers followed the side of her body, to the base of her stomach, to the top of her hair line, down through her wetness. He stubbed out their cigarettes. She trembled again, shook once as if chilled, and he brought her shoulders and face to him and held her, never wanting to leave this room.

Sutton climbed down off the train and walked into the village of Bassingbourn.

Five minutes past five and his head was clear again. He had slept off the booze on the train up from London, wondering about the faulty fuel pump, recalling the *Doats*—spurts of memory, flashes of Page, things he said, his voice counting off something in the cockpit during some old training run he'd been on with Sutton.

He crossed the pavement.

A half-block away a Jaguar sports car turned the corner and slipped to a halt near the curbstone. The door opened; long slim legs came out.

Crashing *The Lazy Lady* wasn't luck, Sutton knew that. Some had said Sutton was lucky coming back across the Channel after four direct hits and cannon fire from two fighters. But he'd never been a lucky guy. He had manhandled the bomber, outfoxed her; he had piloted a dying ship. Someone else, perhaps Page in those very last seconds, might've waited for luck to make a pass. A benevolent gesture one might deem opportune in a moment of crisis. Airplanes, his father had told him, don't wait to have luck kiss them; they insist pilots fly them.

A tall young woman quickly stepped away from the Jaguar. Her steps were neat, hasty, and she disappeared into a bakery.

"It's all hard work and hard luck," his father had told him while they were banging an oil-line into shape on some heap they had to have back in the air that afternoon. "Don't expect anything else—if you do, you're going to be one disappointed puppy."

Irontail would make it hard; would lecture him about the war effort and how he and the United States of America needed every muscle from every pilot every minute of every day. He would use Chrisp and Griffin as examples. "If there were only a few knights of the air," Parker had confided in Cole once, "Chrisp and Griffin would certainly be sitting at the head of the table—near me."

Sutton glanced at his watch: six past five. The Liege milk-run would be over, and the crews would be landing.

The woman came through the doorway with a package, walking as quickly as she had a few moments ago when she entered the shop. When Sutton bumped into her the package fell and two rolls bounced onto the sidewalk like baseballs. "Oh, I . . ." She was startled, hadn't seen him coming. He apologized and bent over for the rolls.

The woman was slim and tall. Slight breasts were vaguely outlined under a willowy white polka-dot dress that fluttered, pressing her narrow hips. A boyish figure with ice-blue eyes, her champagne-colored hair was cut straight at her shoulders.

He put the rolls into the paper bag and she thanked him and walked around the rear of the car and opened the driver's door and slid in. She began searching through an expensive handbag for the keys, which were hanging in the ignition.

"May I ask you your name?" Sutton said politely, through the passenger window.

"I'm sorry, but I am rather in a hurry."

"I would just like to apologize for—"

"You have done that."

"I'm stationed here at the air base and perhaps I could, we could have a drink, dinner, maybe you could use some butter or nylons. I—"

"I don't need anything, thank you."

She cleared out most of the bag: a thin wallet, a small leather-bound phone book with gold Gothic initials, a tube of lipstick, a vial of perfume, and a gold cigarette case.

Half-remembering, half-wishing, Sutton said, "I've seen you before. You and this car go very well together." He eyed the keys.

She didn't smile; she gave nothing away. This was a serious woman, edgy, fidgeting through a handbag with quick but graceful movements. Her polished nails flashed maroon in the fading sunlight. "I never come to the village." Her dress slid to mid-thigh; her trim legs reflected off the wind-screen.

Sutton said, "Once. You have to have

been through once, and that's when I saw you — in this car — your hair blowing in the wind, and you were driving very fast and you looked like you look now. Serious."

"I always drive fast."

"You shouldn't." He poked his head through the window. Her scent was in the car: rose powder mixed with rich leather upholstery. "I asked myself if I'd ever see you again because, well, you know how seldom you see a person, a stranger that you think is . . . beautiful."

She took the handbag in both hands and opened it over the seat and everything fell: a few slips of paper, a white handkerchief, a gold pen attached to a fragile gold chain. There was nothing left.

He stuck his hand out and turned the ignition and the engine fired. "Needs a tuneup," he said. Her head jerked around and she threw it back and went tight with anger — not at him, at herself, for forgetting. "You rush too much," Sutton said.

She scooped up the handbag's contents and said, "And you should be more careful walking down the sidewalk, Captain."

"You should have dinner with me."

"No."

"Will you have a drink with me?"

"No."

"Will you take a walk with me?"

"No."

"Would you like a ride in a fast B-17?"

133

"Not at all, thank you. I hate airplanes."
She had everything back into the bag. Her hair fell across her face.

"What *would* you like?"

She snapped the clasp and placed the handbag neatly against her narrow hip and tossed her silky hair away from her face and threw an arm over the back of the passenger seat. She faced Sutton, her cold, crisp blue eyes dazzling him, her lips still drawn tight from anger. Her face was half in shadow, the other half lit with soft pink light, and her legs were parted slightly. Between them there was silence but something was said. She did not want to say anything; she didn't want to tell him anything. She didn't want to hear her own words. But loneliness makes you do things that otherwise you would not ordinarily do. Her foot searched the clutch, and she opened the passenger door and said softly: "Get in."

He slammed the door and she put the Jaguar in first and the tires screamed, spilling the rolls on the thick carpet.

Neither of them spoke as the Jaguar beat through sheets of rain. She drove to her house.

The place was hidden, enveloped on one hundred acres of manicured lawns and trees.

It was a baronial Tudor home constructed before the First World War, and it contained a solarium and an impeccable garden with roses that bloomed to the size of brandy glasses. The den was filled with memorabilia from the British 10th Hussars, the Prince of Wales's own Royal Troopers dating back to the Second Afghan War in 1879. The room had the smell of gun oil and valor, a good masculine smell, and glittered with gold and silver decorations and colorful but muted battle ribbons. The billiard room was octagonal. The living room was elegant and sunken. The master bedroom suite contained two fireplaces, two bathrooms, and a large poster bed carved from slabs of solid English oak. The library was stacked with leatherbound books which the woman had read between moments of sorrow and shattering loss. The house had been willed to her late husband by her father-in-law; then her husband was killed just before the Battle of Britain.

It was a peaceful place stained with loneliness.

The woman's name was Arianne, and in the darkened foyer Sutton brought his arms around her rain-soaked dress and kissed her lips. With closed eyes she took his shoulders into her hands and pressed him gently against her trembling body. They had come to the house in haste, hoping to lose for a time the sadness that had been a part of each of them.

"I must get out of this wet dress," she said, sounding rather proper. She pointed to the living room. "Make yourself a drink."

"I'll wait for you," he said.

Minutes later she returned in a burgundy robe with a wide, tightly drawn sash. She placed a magnum of champagne on the butler's table and poured two glasses. Her movements were smooth, sure, her hands graceful, and her eyes gave her away. She was a strong woman without self-pity, and she had used this strength to hide her pain. Without courage she would be coiled in the corner of some mental hospital, half-forgotten.

She offered him a glass and he said, "Are you trying to get me skunked?"

She threw her head back the way she had in the car and they clinked glasses and her soft eyes caught his. "You are old enough to do that yourself," she answered, moving to a record player in the corner of the room. In a moment she had the thing spinning and a sweet trumpet filled the place.

The notes were true and familiar, and when she sat again on the couch, Sutton guessed: "Bunny Berigan—1936?"

Her lopsided grin said yes.

I Can't Get Started?"

Another smile.

"I love that record," he said. "It reminds me of hot summer nights sitting on a porch, sipping a Coke and listening to crickets."

The trumpet solo subsided and Berigan began singing.

Sutton took her close and brought his

hand to her cheek and kissed her gently.

> *I've flown around the world in a plane,*
> *Settled revolutions in Spain,*
> *And the North Pole I've charted.*
> *Still I can't get started with you.*

> *On the golf course I'm under par,*
> *Metro-Goldwyn has asked me to star,*
> *I've got a house, a showplace.*
> *Still I can't get no place with you.*

The lyrics reminded him of Allison and her backporch where the sound of crickets filled summer nigts, where her bashful smile disappeared only long enough to take a sip of Coca-Cola and give him a kiss. But that was America and it might have been a million years behind him. This was England and—*oh, Jesus, this girl is beautiful and smells of lilac soap.*

She kissed him and brought him to her breasts as if his weight would force out some ghost that she herself could not unleash.

"Are you a pilot?" she asked.

"Yes. B-17s." He took more champagne, put the glass down and studied the bubbles rising endlessly from the bottom of the hollow stem.

"That," she said, "is Geoffrey." she pointed to a silver-framed photo of a handsome man dressed in the blue uniform of an RAF pilot. "He's my husband."

"Well," Sutton said, looking startled, "perhaps I'm in the wrong place."

"No, you're not." She smiled. "That's all that's left of him. He was a fighter pilot — Spitfires. He loved flying, as I sense you do. And because of that and his lack of fear, he's dead. So, maybe it's love and fear that kills people. He didn't know what fear was. Some men don't know these things, and that's usually only good for them and not the people who love them — the people they leave behind. I think if more of you knew fear there would be less of you dead and the gravediggers would have to earn their keep elsewhere."

"I have a friend, Benny Tutone, who loves war. I'm sure you can't imagine that. He says it's exciting, that you discover who you are, what you're made of. Perhaps that's what your husband was looking for, and maybe that's why he had no fear and why there is such a thing as war — because man is always trying to forget his fears, and you must overcome that if you are to succeed in battle."

She was angry at herself. The last time she'd given herself to a man he was killed. Her breath came shallow, and with it the loneliness of a woman who had lost something — and the fear that she might lose something again.

"When I think," she said, "of how little time we all have and the bloody war that's raging next door . . . I think of the generals—the Yanks, the Brits, the Jerrys—in their gay, pompous uniforms, and how they act like chessmen playing a game with their pawns, tumbling them into box after box." She touched Sutton's arm. "I hate them."

He shrugged his shoulders and searched her eyes. He had a war to fight and a special mission to fly. What she said might be true, he thought—though perhaps a bit too poetic. His reality was in the sky and his only regret was he didn't have time to write poems.

She stood silently for a long moment and then she loosened the sash. Her robe opened; it had been closed long enough.

"It doesn't really matter, though," she said quickly, pulling him up by his hand and leading him towards the bedroom, "because you will never come back, none of you— you're all too bloody innocent and that's why the generals and politicians rule the world."

In the bedroom, the robe slipped to her feet.

Thunder rolled off the hard oak walls.

She padded over to the chaise lounge and lay there, her long arms over the back as she watched him undress. A flash of lightning ignited her skin and the rain-spattered panes threw an eerie light on her smallish breasts and lean legs.

After a few seconds she rose and walked to

the bed, naked, and they held each other and listened to the thunder banging over the roof. Her flesh was cool, fresh, with out a ripple or flaw. Her eyes were half-open, and she smiled at him. He moved his hands over her body, as if to stoke the coolness into fire, stroking her shoulders, her breasts, her abdomen. Before his hand reached her sex, her legs opened slightly. She sighed and said something, but the thunder kept it from him.

Her hair was disheveled, cast over the pillow like a fan of straw, and her breathing came quicker, more shallow, as his fingers explored. She could have lived for this if she wanted to—for sex, for men. She knew the tension, the yearning of unsatisfied desire, the hunger and turmoil that raged; the long nights, naked, rubbing herself, primed for orgasm that only a man could bring. Too many nights had been spend passionately exploring herself, without full release of the tension that was present. Instead, she waited for the right time. Sutton was very gentle; he cared for her pleasure, and she felt this. The selfishness of other men, their desire to tend to themsleves, was something distant now.

Her tension swelled, suffused, then focused under his motioning fingers rubbing her thickening lips. She wanted to move against it, to engulf it, to tease then satisfy herself. The pleasure of having something there, his hand, a new sensation, had almost been forgotten. The sweet warm touch, the tease, was more than she could bear. She rubbed her sex against his hand, closed her eyes and focused on the movement, the one pressing the other, slowly.

"Please . . . oh . . . please."

He slid down, as if to pay homage to her feet, slipping his hands along her skin, flushed and warm. Her heart beat wildly, tapped against her chest. He whispered something, then took her roseate nipple between his lips; her breasts were like those of a young girl. He pressed against her, engulfed her, smothered her body, her pretty face, pushing gently, then violently. She felt his hard sex sawing against hers and she wanted to yell out, to tell him to take her; but she waited and teased herself again, half-hoping he would wait longer—until she could not bear the tension. She wanted to explode.

He moved up and then under and the tip slipped in, then halted. It lingered there and she savored its weight, its presence, his moisture against hers, mingling like their frantic kisses.

"Please," she said softly. He stirred again, moved, and she parted her legs further. But he remained still, sensing her desire to prolong the excruciating pleasure. Her palms went wet and her skin turned moist, and the idea of having him, engulfing him and retaining him, was her whole focus. "Oh please."

"Arianne," he said, savoring the name, the sound of it against the rain and thunder. "Arianne," he repeated once more, feeling something so deep in his soul that it frightened him. He lost control, because a sensation new to him swept through his limbs, his heart and soul.

He moved again, and the more he did this, the more aware she was of her emptiness, the deep void that had to be filled. Electricity pulsed through her, fluttering her womb until she thought she would run out of air and become breathless and die in his arms, under him. He pushed deeper. Her wet flesh yeiled, the moisture opening her like a dewy flower.

"My God! My God!"

In a second she was moving, dwelling on each sensation, meeting him. Her breath came faster and faster until her soul seemed to abandon her body, and her legs and arms tensed and quivered. She opened her mouth, silently revealing her hunger. He plunged deeped and deeper, and with each motion she countered and drove herself to meet him.

"Oh God!"

The sensation made her jerk. "Oh please . . . please don't . . . stop." He took her head and locked his mouth on hers, but the scream of her climax escaped. Her head rolled back and forth, from side to side, and her legs came back and grabbed him with a profound fury.

After a few long moments she rested motionless and crosslegged alongside him, the muted light accenting her square-jawed face. She stayed there in silence, staring at him, glad for what she'd done.

"Good?"

"Very."

The only sounds were the taps of rain beating the glass, hammering the leaves. She walked to the dresser after a few minutes, tossing her hair back, running her hands down her slim legs, glad for what she had done. She disappeared in a veil of shadow then returned and sat next to him and lit a cigarette.

Thunder rolled and faded then cracked and returned with a deep tremble. He brought his arms up and drew her down and kissed her cheek, happy to be here.

CHAPTER NINE

For a long time there had been nothing but silence, and the silence had spread everywhere. Not just at the base of the tower here at Bassingbourn, but beyond it.

Light had been going dimmer and the sun's red disc was smeared pink through boiling clouds. To the west the sky was awash in saffron. To the east there was a wall of blue-gray cloth. The sky no longer beamed and the earth no longer glittered. The Channel had turned an ashen death against a froth of endless whitecaps. Soon the sun would be gone and there would be rain.

Up and down the coast a warning had been posted.

At 5:06, Sergeant Cole and Colonel Parker could hear the engines of *This Is It!* popping in the distance. Through the binoculars the bomber was a thin black dash outlined against a blackening sky—a thin feather of white smoke marked the flight path, turning now for Bassingbourn's runway.

"I think Chrisp's ship has been hit," Parker said, sighting through the binoculars.

Cole brought his glasses down and squinted. "Doesn't sound too good."

Ground personnel stood around the tower, hair, skirts, coveralls bannering in the stiff breeze. They'd been waiting a half-hour, hoping, reciting forgotten prayers. Fire trucks and bicycles rolled down the field when the first bomber was spotted, and now more planes appeared on the horizon, below the clouds; they were a long way off, skimming the earth's curve. Someone counted aloud: "One . . . three . . . eight . . . thirteen . . . sixteen. . . ."

Flares from Very pistols announced the wounded and dead.

Chrisp had released his bombs over the general area designated as *the target*. They had been given maps of it, they had coordinates for it, they had heard the logistics of it, and yet they were uncertain about hitting it or missing it. They might have hit children, sure; they might have hit hospitals, sure; they might have destroyed art; they might have scored on grandmothers and grandfathers; they might have wounded bakers and tailors, lawyers and doctors, street bums or whores; they might have killed cats and cattle, sure; they might've killed a priest hearing confession; or two lovers making love. No one was certain. Except the people near *the target*.

The bombers had been humping along like big fat buses with heavy loads when the nightmare appeared.

Chrisp wasn't surprised. He was startled.

The nightmare was a group of forty-nine German fighters; wasp bees with stingers flashing through the stratosphere.

Chrisp muttered, "Oh shit," because there was nothing else to do but sit and fly. There were Fw-190s and Me-109s from an assortment of squadrons, and their numbers made them unusually bold, incisive. They'd sprung up ninety-three seconds after the B-17s dropped their loads. Their Prussian efficiency had failed; they had been given the wrong coordinates. If not, they would have been diving into the formation before it reached Liege. They had cut through in echelon left and right, in staggered and line-abreast formations, singularly and in pairs and groups of threes and fours. Blistering machine gun fire from the Forts met them immediately. But that wasn't enough to stop the nightmare.

Wicked Wanda merely disappeared in a huge white flash of crazy broiling flame and gas smoke. Burning chunks smeared the sky, and there were no chutes. *Joe-Joe* dove like a shovel—it fell straight in a screaming dive, and there were no chutes. They had punched the fourth bomber, *Lucy,* from the port and starboard directions, three seconds apart. Cannon fire holed the ship's wings and pierced the gas tanks with incendiary fire at the wing-root section. A snarling flame erupted into a ball of orange and red rays and then there was a terrific explosion that shattered the air and the ship caved into itself, broke into four distinct parts and dropped. And there were no chutes.

Chrisp's ship took thirty-eight 20mm hits—nine and a half pounds of steel and high explosives. One shattered the catwalk truss. Others passed through the hydraulic pump panel, accumulators, and servicing valves. The most damaging exploded through the sump drain on the number one engine; it soon began to overheat, but not enough to prevent a safe return to base.

Coming back into Bassingbourn the *Prissy Missy* had two engines out and three dead crewmen. And then she ran into the ultimate problem—she had no pilot; she was a dying bird about to crash because of a lack of flying talent.

The copilot had been killed when a shred of metal from the windscreen framing blew off and pierced his throat. His heart pumped out blood until he died. The pilot had been hit in the chest with a chunk of the servo-motor that operated the turret. A cannon round shattered it and banged it around the cockpit at nearly two hundred miles an hour before it slammed into his chest less than a second later. He was on the flooring, foaming blood, gurgling. He made insane sounds and reached for the throttle quadrant.

Sergeant Turlow, the turret gunner and flight engineer, had taken position in the left seat and had the control column in his hands. He'd never flown a plane before.

When they passed the English coast three crewmen elected to bail out. It was a wise choice.

A P-51 Mustang fighter flown by Maj. Mack Mestinger was sent up and flanked them. "Teddy Bear to Shotgun Two," He said, referring to *Prissy Missy's* radio call, "do you copy? Over."

There was confusion on the radio now and the remaining crew members aboard *Prissy Missy* began talking at once:

"Shit!"

"Who's that?"

"Get off the fuckin' radio, asshole!"

"Bananas to you motherfucker."

"Listen for shit's sake," Mestinger yelled, "this is Teddy Bear. I want to land you guys, I want to give you instructions!" Mestinger was a dapper gent with a sweeping handlebar mustache and he was rated in most Air Force aircraft. He flapped his wings. "Do you see me? Look out your port side fellas, I'm right here."

"Hey, Turlow—out there on the left—a Mustang."

"Oh."

Colonel Parker, monitoring the channel from the Bassingbourn tower, only added to the confusion. "This is Foxhound here, Colonel Parker to Teddy—"

"This is Teddy Bear to Shotgun Two, do you—"

"This is Colonel Parker—"

"Will you get the fuck off the radio!" someone yelled.

"Everybody shut up," Turlow said, "I'm trying to listen to "

"Oh balls," a crewman in the bomber said in frustration.

"Settle down, settle down," Mestinger said.

"Okay."

"Ah . . . this it Teddy Bear to Shotgun Two. Are you copying?"

"Affirmative," Turlow responded. "Got you five by five."

"All right, now," Mestinger said, flying ten feet off the *Prissy Missy's* port wingtip, "who's flying the airplane?"

"I am, Sergeant Turlow."

"What is the status of your pilot, Sergeant?" asked Mestinger.

"His status is he's almost dead. He's bleeding badly."

"I'm the flight engineer," said Turlow rapidly, "and I've never flown one of these birds except to hold it straight and level. Landing's something I haven't done. I can fly in circles all day but when the juice's gone, that's it, Jack."

"Well, we'll get you guys down," Mestinger said. "Believe me." He sounded like he meant it, that it would happen.

"Yeah, sure," Turlow whispered.

"My ass," one of the crewmen added.

For the next twenty minutes Turlow took flying lessons. He learned flap positions, stall speeds, rate of descent, power settings, angle of attack, coordination between throttle and control column and foot pedals, trim setting. What took pilots months to learn, Turlow was trying to cram into twenty small minutes. He sensed it was impossible.

"Okay," Mestinger said. "Let's take a crack at it. Remember what I told you about the throttle setting—too little and you stall and go down like a rock."

The *Prissy Missy* was lined up with the runway, descending, the nose begging to go down. Ambulances and fire trucks dotted the field.

"When I tell you, nose below the horizon, throttle all the way back."

"I think I want a refund on my ticket," someone said in the interphone. "Where's the stewardess? Oh, miss, miss. . . ."

At three hundred feet the cows and birds sensed that the *Prissy Missy* wouldn't make it.

"Pull up! More throttle! Throttle forward!" Mestinger yelled.

"Fuck me!"

"Oh shit!"

The ship rose, gaining altitude.

Mestinger said, "Listen. I just heard from Colonel Parker on B channel. He feels—and so do I—that you guys should bail out. Take it up to about six thousand feet and jump. It's the best way, then you—"

Parker interrupted. "Sergeant Turlow, this is Colonel Parker here, do you copy?"

"Roger."

"We feel it would be best if you all bailed out. Don't, I repeat, don't try to land the ship."

Thirty seconds passed, then a minute, then a minute and a half. Mestinger asked, "Turlow? What the hell's going on?"

Silence.

"Turlow!"

"Listen, Major," Turlow finally said. "We took a vote and everyone's bailing out except me and Cohen here in the copilot's seat. We're going to give it another shot."

"That's really no good, fella. Bailing out's the way to go."

"Negative."

"Why?"

"Well, we think the lieutenant can make it if we get him down to a doctor. He's unconscious. He can't bail out. If we leave we might as well kill him right now. The others are going to start jumping."

Mestinger said, "If you crash that plane,

Sergeant, three men will die. If you bail out, only one man does."

"Would you like us to leave you if we thought you had a chance?"

Mestinger hesitated for a second. "No. I guess not."

Turlow brought the *Prissy Missy* up to six thousand feet. Two falling objects blossomed into parachutes, the only ones on this day of the Liege run. Then he brought the ship around and headed back to the runway.

"What would you like me to do?" Cohen asked Turlow.

"Talk about screwing. How would you like to screw Rita Hayworth?"

"Wow!"

"Yeah, I know. Remember *National Velvet* with Elizabeth Taylor?"

"Yeah."

"Remember the horse?"

"Yeah. I think."

"When she got off the horse, that's when I would've like to have screwed her. Right then and there."

"Christ, Turlow, you are an odd ball. How 'bout just flyin' this bitch and stop talkin' about broads."

"You wanted to know what you could do."

"Right."

"Well—"

"Okay—remember that dame, Mona? You used to refer to her as the London cookie; the one with the cow tits, you used to say."

"Yeah, the one with the big balloons." Turlow smiled.

"I fucked her."

"You are a lying asshole, Cohen."

"No, I'm not."

"Where?"

"In the vagina!"

"That's not what I mean."

"In her parent's living room," said Cohen. He looked down at the crowd and continued: "Her mom and dad were in the bedroom listening to Brahms and we were humping on the carpet and I got sore elbows and sore knees—carpet rash. When she saw it she laughed. She said she loved uniforms, and that she was doing it for her mother country because we Yanks were doing so much for her. You know something," he said, looking down at the crowd again, "they look like they're waiting for something awful to happen."

"Don't look down. Keep shootin' me some more jive."

"Turlow," Cohen said, looking at his friend, "I just want you to know that I'm not the kind of guy who would've told you that. I mean, I wouldn't've unless . . . unless this—"

"You are indeed shooting me jive, Cohen, and you know I know it."

Cohen put his hand on Turlow's shoulder.

"Do me a favor. Just land this bitch so I can go back and get more carpet rash."

Hats had blown off the crowd and no one went after them. Parker and Cole watched through the binoculars as *Prissy Missy* made her steep descent.

"Too steep," Parker murmured.

The crowd was silent. They listened to the banging engines, out of syncy, jerky. A nurse began to cry.

"Turlow," said Cohen. "It does not appear that you are doing such a hot fucking job with this airplane."

"You're right, but it was one hell of a try."

The *Prissy Missy* impacted at 240 MPH and exploded into a thick dome of flame that spilled seven hundred yards down the runway, leaving a river of burning fuel and cracking ammunition that spit into the air. And then it stopped and burned with a roar that lasted for a long time.

The Liege milk-run had ended.

CHAPTER TEN

"Hey, boss," Tutone said, throwing his gear into the forward hatch, "we going to get some Germans today?"

"Yeah, and we're going to end the war before dinner," Sutton said.

For good luck, Tutone reached up and patted *The Beast* on the nose section. The words had been drawn in bright yellow bubble-style letters, outlined with brilliant red. Below the two-foot-high letters was an aardvark-like creature in green with a small set of stubby white wing. Fire-breathing red bullets spewed from the machine gun-shaped nostrils. The eyes, however, appeared soft and understanding.

Today *The Beast* was going on her first raid.

Tutone was so wild with excitement that he had a difficult time hoisting himself through the forward hatch. On the ground and in the air, he was one person: warrior, knight of the skies, whose sole purpose was to destroy the enemy. He was an up-tempo kid from the streets of New York where there had been no purpose, no meaning, no chance for glory. But here he'd found a place for himself. He had a mission today instead of another training flight, and his only dread was that the war would end before he could make his mark. When he heard he'd be part of today's raid—a run over Brest—he let out a whoop with the same verve and energy he'd give watching DiMaggio smack a grand slam with two outs in the bottom of the ninth.

After he muscled through the hatch, Bo Baker banged into Tutone. "Hey, Bo," Tutone said, grabbing Baker's elbow, "I shacked up with a cookie in London last night and she asked me what I thought about the war. I told her that we're all part of history, that we destroy and that is our work and that I love it. No one in the history of mankind has been more destructive than us, Bo. Ain't that terrific?"

Baker screwed up his face and thought for a second, then he said, slowly: "I think that's a load of horseshit." He excused himself, disappearing into the radio room.

In the cockpit, Griffin was unusually quiet, almost pensive. He appeared out of place in his pressed shirt and tie, his creased trousers and white silk scarf.

Sutton buckled into the pilot's seat. He'd heard about Roger's encounter with T.R.

"Heard you got your ass painted black last night, Rog."

"Something happened to the stove."

"Yeah, T.R.'s what happened to the stove."

· When the Chief plugged in his interphone jack something spiritual came over him. A seriousness marred his face, changed it into a sullen mask that drew his eyes darker, deeper into his skull. He took a deep breath. He felt nervous waiting for the engines to crank over.

Gibson the navigator assured Sutton and Griffin that he knew his way around Europe. Navigational aids were turning into a sophisticated science. The days of dead-reckoning and sticking a wet finger into the wind were gone forever. This was the age of radar, Lorenze radio beams, and jamming signals. Gibson knew what each of them did. He knew their tricks, their failings, and their strengths. He was a navigational fanatic. Gibson loved electronic wizardry the way most men love women. But he still hadn't gained the crew's full confidence; they thought he was finicky.

U-boat pens were down as the target at Brest, which is on the outermost western lip of the French coast. The land base it rests on juts out between the English Channel and the Bay of Biscay. Hours after the mission was announced, Gibson had the route memorized. He knew the topography surrounding the target better than any other navigator in the Group.

During the early morning hours the Fortresses had been loaded with bombs. Operations, intelligence, navigators and bombardiers, weather and communications, were planned out and made into a unified pattern. After an 0830 briefing the Group was prepared.

This Is It! rested next to *The Beast's* starboard wing. Before Tutone climbed through the hatch he yelled at Chrisp's waist gunner, pointing to the ship's name: "Hey, Charlie! That ain't it! This here is it!" Then he gave the gunner the finger. He waved it at the end of his outstretched hand for a few seconds.

The waist gunner stuck his head through the window and returned the sign. "Fuck you!" he yelled back.

Kid Kiley saw the waist gunner as he pulled one of *The Beast's* props around; he muttered one word: "Motherfucker."

The morning mist was gone. The sky was a white map of puffy cloud and soft gold light.

In the village of Bassingbourn a parson unlocked the heavy wooden door of his fourteenth-century chancel, then he stretched and gathered in the vision of fresh daylight. A 19-year-old maiden with slight, fragile features rose from her soapy bath water and disregarded her towel and walked to the full-length mirror and studied her glistening form. A widow glanced at a photo of her dead soldier husband and wept silently. An innkeeper stacked bottles of fresh ale; a rooster crowed; a baby cried; an old man stuffed a worn *Meerschaum* pipe, applied a flame and sucked. On a nearby hill a sycamore drooped sadly and was stirred by a gentle breeze.

Near the village square the clock sang once; 8:30.

A flare shot from the control tower and tore the fresh sky.

Engines coughed as four ships fired their engines simultaneously: *Naughty Nancy, The City of Chicago, Pistol Packin' Patty,* and *Erotic Neurotic.* Clouds of blue exhaust smoke billowed and whirled from rust-brown exhaust stacks. Then the earth vibrated.

Sutton gave the command and *The Beast's* engines churned. *This Is It!* followed immediately, and then *Mona Wona's* props were churning. Now there were twenty B-17s prepared to takeoff. The sound was heard miles away.

Today Colonel Parker would be flying copilot for Chrisp in *This Is It!* Bob Len of *The New York Times* would be flying with them, doing a four-part series on the Air Force in Europe.

This Is It! was the first to taxi. *The Beast, Mona Wona, Chattanooga Chew Chew, Spot Remover, Say It Isn't So,* and *Air*

Hound, lumbered behind.

The parson brought his arm down and cocked his head toward the clamor on the horizon. He closed his eyes and offered a simple prayer; he asked God to bring them all back safely. The 19-year-old maiden ran her hands up to her rigid nipples; she rubbed them then glanced through the leaded panes of the bathroom window. The noise momentarily disturbed her sexual reverie. The widow kept her face locked in her trembling hands; tears burned her warm cheeks. Ale bottles rattled. The innkeeper cursed the Yankee airmen and the preposterous racket they made. The old man continued sucking his pipe. The rooster dashed toward a short bush. Surprised, the baby stared wide-eyed and silent at the ceiling where it thought the sound came from.

Chrisp slid his throttles up and *This Is It!* rolled down the runway. Airborne, it passed over the spot where Page had died.

Sutton's hands pressed the throttles forward and the crew felt *The Beast* surge down the runway. The engines worked smoothly, lifting them higher and higher.

Tutone smiled and Griffin eyed the vibrating instruments. The Chief sighed with relief, still not certain this was a good ship. Murmuring a Hail Mary, Kid Kiley sat in the tail gunner's compartment and watched the earth grow smaller and smaller, the shape of Bassingbourn going less distinct.

Bush was anxious; he unraveled a stick of Wrigley's gum and felt a film of sweat around his large neck. Bo Baker, detached and calm, continued reading his book. Gibson noted the takeoff time: 0837 by his Air Force issued chronometer.

It took the Group forty-five minutes to form over the Channel, a feat more treacherous than combat. This was especially true in foul weather when the possibility of crashing into another bomber was very likely. But today the Group was silhouetted against a base of furrowed and rippled cloud that spread to the horizon. The bombers turned southwest and sped toward Brest where they would spill out their bomb load on the U-boat pens, turn, and head back to England. On paper—and during Parker's briefing—the raid appeared simple, because Brest was such a short distance from the English coast.

"Just a jump across the puddle," Parker told them, slicing his pointer up and down the large map. He was actually trying to console himself because every time he flew a mission he was nervous and anxious. Raids were a paradox for Parker. He needed them for advancement, but he was fearful of combat; he dreaded it. He took a mission like a sick man takes an enema. Everybody in the Group knew this, but he kept it from his superiors at Wing.

When the Group was halfway to Brest,

Parker broke radio silence and began his drill instructor routine, demanding that the formation be flown by the book, tighter, with more diligence and effort. He did this for the benefit of *The New York Times* reporter, who apparently didn't see or hear anything because he was in the radio room vomiting. It wasn't until they got within ten miles of Brest that he straightened up and took his first peek.

The mission was flown at eight thousand feet, which didn't thrill anyone. Instead of going over the target at a safer 15,000, where the flak would be less accurate, Parker insisted that this lower flight level would give the Group "more integrity" on the target. It also meant that more men would be wounded. Eight thousand feet over the target and back home. Not a foot higher, and certainly not a foot lower.

This altitude gave everyone in *The Beast* a bad case of the willies. They knew that it would take the German fighters less time after scrambling to reach them, and they would be low enough for accurate sighting from flak guns. They bitched about it with more regularity as the raid progressed until Sutton had to tell them to shut up.

Sutton pressed his mike button. "Gunners, test your guns, and don't shoot any of our own guys down." Each gunner gave a quick burst and the ship rattled like a palsied animal. Tutone and Skolinsky continued to slowly spin their turrets, scanning the sky for Germans. Below, the cloud base vanished and the English Channel was visible.

A gunner in *Pucker Up* called out an enemy fighter formation. "There's about twenty-five of 'em comin' in from eight o'clock," he said, rather calmly.

The Beast's gunners focused on the advancing fighters, which had split into two groups and were coming rapidly toward the bombers' formation. The Germans had learned that their best attack was head-on. Now, their first sweeps were made at the lead bomber. *Pucker Up's* gunners worked furiously, firing at each fighter formation as they came in wave after wave. The fighters were all over the sky, coming in from port and starboard, fore and aft. Two of them became bold and attacked *The New York Clipper;* she fell over to her right and dove toward the Channel in a straight line.

"No chutes!" shouted Tutone; then a second later one appeared, then two, four, seven, eight, nine.

"We got dinner guests," the Chief announced calmly into the interphone, aiming his .50-caliber at two Fw-190s coming down from eleven o'clock. Their bellies were pale blue and gray. Skolinsky and Tutone swept their guns around and fired with the Chief. The five .50s jerked with jackhammer force. Three lines of white tracer rounds converged on the lead fighter but he juked at the last second. "Son-of-a-bitch, we missed 'em!" someone yelled. Griffin said something unintelligible then the interphone jammed with voices. Tutone cursed and smashed his fist into his thigh. Another fighter passed below Skolinsky's tracers, which were a hundred yards off target.

An Fw-190 came head-on and Sutton shouted out his position.

Rowe worked the handles controlling the Bendix chin-turret and Tutone fired, each of them firing a three-second burst. Skolinsky fired but missed; he watched the fighter slip past the last squadron.

In a battle situation, Griffin was supposed to be in charge of interphone discipline and fire control. But in reality no one was in charge of anything. The moment the fighters appeared no one crewman could see all the sectors of fire, so it became a free-for-all. Each man had his own zone. Tutone's was ahead and below. Skolinsky searched ten o'clock to two o'clock, below. The Chief, in the right waist, searched two to four, high and low. Bush, on the left, eight to ten, high and low. Rowe, with the chin turret, had nine to three, ahead. The plan was to keep your zone and call in a fighter as soon as you spotted one. Griffin would coordinate the shooting. This was neat in practice but when the real thing came along *The Beast's* crew shot it to hell because they were so hell-bent on thinking of themselves, instead of thinking like a team. The greatest danger was to the ship's efficiency and self-protection. No one kept his mouth shut. During this moment, rank and personality was meaningless, and the crew was supposed to come together as one force, one mind. But it didn't work. Sutton knew this and he was angry.

The Germans were organized today. They showed bravery without being stupid. Two of them worked together like ballet dancers. They came around the outer periphery of Sutton's squadron. Tutone kept his turret locked on them. The Germans were at full-throttle flying first abreast of *The Beast* until they disappeared, then coming head-on. Griffin howled their position and Tutone leveled his guns where he thought they'd be. He couldn't see them. Suddenly they appeared. The German guns flickered. At seven hundred yards they split, one going starboard, the other port. Before he fired, the starboard German was hit by a wall of machine gun fire from another B-17. The fighter vanished in a cloud of firelight. Two seconds later a wing blew off and the craft quivered and rolled over. Then it lumbered like a sick bird and dove for the Channel. A long tongue of flame followed. The fighter pilot was burned dead before the ship impacted, trapped by a broken canopy release.

The Germans broke off their attack once the Group passed the coastline. The pens were in sight and then the flak began. It was surprisingly inaccurate. On runs like this, the Germans would attack with fighters, follow up with flak and try to disperse the formation, then once the bombs were away, the fighters would return. But these batteries were either sleeping or had insufficient time to bracket their shots.

"See anything?" Sutton asked the crew over the interphone.

"Yeah," Rowe said. "A peaceful French town."

Everyone watched the pens coming up and a few moments later they salvoed their bombs. The Group began its slow turn away from the smoking target and Skolinsky screamed something into the interphone. The crew followed his directions and looked ahead and below.

Air Hound had come under *Moonlight Moanin'* and had caught a bomb on the tail section. The aircraft was spiraling earthward in a large lazy circle—a fish without a tail spinning toward the ocean floor.

"Oh Christ," Baker said. "After all this they're going down because of a stupid accident."

Three weeks ago the same thing happened on another raid but the ship managed to land safely. Today was different.

"The bomb must've exploded," added Baker.

No one spotted chutes. The centrifugal force had kept them prisoners.

The fighters didn't return. Tutone was disappointed. As the flak continued, he began to berate the other gunners' inaccuracy. An argument broke loose, and Sutton told them all to shut up. The Chief was about to reply when they heard a sharp crack, like a two-by-four snapping. *The Beast* heaved up, tilted starboard. When Sutton gained control Bo Baker announced that the port inboard engine had taken a direct hit. The engine billowed black smoke and the prop was windmilling. Suddenly, the engine shuddered and tried to free itself from the bolted mounts. The vibration swept through *The Beast's* airframe.

"Fire in the number two engine," Baker announced calmly. "We've got a fire in—"

"We heard you!" Sutton interrupted. He ordered Griffin to turn the ignition off.

"Hit the feathering switch."

Griffin pressed the switch while Sutton turned the ignition switch to "engine off." The number two engine throttle was closed and the cowl flaps were shut. Sutton trimmed the plane and turned on the automatic flight control.

"Is anybody hurt?" he asked.

Negative responsed came through his headset.

The shell, an 88mm, had come up from a seventy-five degree angle. The primer had been seated improperly and failed to explode when it slammed into the engine, lessening the damage. Griffin had punched the number two fire extinguisher switch. This activated the cylinder, which contained forty nine pounds of methyl bromide and pressurized by seven pounds of nitrogen. When the cylinder's solenoid snapped the nitrogen released the methyl bromide and the fire was extinguished. The 65,000-pound airplane maintained altitude and airspeed and kept pace with the Group. Baker radioed Parker.

Sutton glanced out the window again and turned quickly to Griffin. "I told you to hit the feathering switch! The damned prop is still windmilling."

"I already did."

Sutton turned back to the engine. There was severe drag; the engine was angled down ten degrees. Then the shuddering came back.

"The number two's smoking again, Captain."

A thin wisp of black smoke began to trail, stemming from the closed cowls. A bright white light shone instantly within the cowls, the tongues of flame began bannering in the slipstream.

"Fire! The number two's on fire," Sutton said. The friction from the turning prop had ignited the cylinders.

"There's no more juice in the fire bottle," Griffin said.

"Pilot to crew, pilot to crew," Sutton

barked, "prepare to abandon the aircraft."

The flames grew longer, enveloping the engine; the prop continued its lazy windmilling.

Griffin suddenly turned to Sutton, and with a note of fear in his voice he said, "What are you going to do?"

Sutton appeared surprised. The dashing Roger Griffin afraid? A few seconds passed, then he said: "That engine's hung on there with four main bolts. It looks like the top two have sheared. If we snap the other two, the engine will fall off like a rock." Then he rocked the wings and the engine bounced slightly but remained. "Damn fucking thing!" He rocked the wings again as fast as he could, but the engine held on. The flames fed back like long orange ribbons.

"I'm going to jump now," Griffin said. He began unbuckling his harness and Sutton reached out and slapped his hands off the buckles. "You ain't doing a thing until I tell you," he said, his brown eyes glaring.

"We're with you, boss," Tutone said.

"I'm going to dive it," said Sutton. "That's the last chance. If we don't get it off soon the fire will hit the wing tanks." He quickly checked the vibrating altimeter: nine thousand feet. "Pilot to crew. I'm going to dive the plane and try to get the engine off. When we gather enough airspeed, I'm going to pull it up and hope the engine snaps off." He pressed the control column forward the

The Beast nosed over.

Eighty five hundred feet.

The airspeed increased: 190, 200, 210.

Eight thousand.

Sutton's hands were frozen on the wheel.

Seventy five hundred.

That's what this war was: discovering yourself, finding your limits.

Seven thousand feet.

It told you who you were, how strong you were, how pitiful you could be when faced with the spirit down there inside your soul, the spirit of fear that would tell you what you really were made of. He faced himself as he never had before and his hands were frozen on the controls because he'd seen the limit of his fear, an impassable steel fence that would not allow him forward nor back. Would Arianne think less of him if he couldn't pull the ship up? Would she laugh at him if he crashed into the Channel? He heard her voice, *It doesn't really matter because you will never come back, none of you—you're all too bloody innocent.* . . . She was standing there in the cockpit, behind him, watching his frozen hands controlled by the spirit of fear. He could not turn to look up at her. It was the fear of seeing himself, who he was, that prevented him, that kept his head fixed. *The wise man has the power*, she had said. Oh how pathetic he was. He hated himself; hated the image reflected in the Plexiglass. He wished her away but she remained. Watching his frozen hands. Waiting for him to do something.

They were going down.

Twenty five hundred feet.

Only Arianne would survive. She would only go so far with him, and then she would dismiss herself and disappear before he ceased to exist.

Two thousand feet.

"Sutton!"

One thousand.

"Sutton for God's sake!" Griffin yelled, "the wings are going to snap off!"

Sutton's hands were sweating, refrigerating his flesh, and he heard Griffin screaming at him, urging him to pull *The Beast* up.

Arianne was leaving them.

Sutton pulled back on the control column. The nose came up and bobbed over the horizon. The pull of gravity had its effect on the engine.

"It's gone!" Baker shouted. "You did it! Jesus you did it.

There was enough power in her frame to keep straight and level; enough airspeed to prevent her from stalling and killing them.

CHAPTER ELEVEN

"Then what happened?"

Sutton jerked back and forth on his chair, tipping it back and forward toward the table, tossing down gulps of Pabst, wondering what Branch Parker, who was happily skunked, was really thinking as he stood there at Sutton's table at the Officers' Club. Arianne, her sparkling hair pulled back over her ears, grinned, delighted that Sutton's ingenuity had saved lives. She pressed his hand, proud to be with him.

"Bloody awful," Sutton said, borrowing a British term. "Blood-eee awful. Everybody was jawing on the interphone wondering if the ship was going to explode, giving their advice; but the mood was pretty calm despite the situation."

Flying back to England on three engines, the Chief had suggested that everyone bail out because he'd never used his parachute and wanted to try it out. Tutone had seemed willing to stay no matter what happened, moving his turret around and looking for Germans. And Kid Kiley kept yelling about how exciting it was getting an engine hit and then dropping it off.

Sutton finished his beer and took up a fresh one. "Generally speaking, Colonel, everybody felt pretty swell in spite of the circumstances." There was one exception— Roger Griffin—but Sutton didn't mention that.

"That's what I like to hear, Captain," Parker said, bringing his hand up. "I salute you." He bobbed, wavering like a grass reed in a stiff breeze. "That's from Rag Tag and me, 'cause we think you did fine . . . I mean a *fine* job."

Sutton and Arianne watched in silence.

T.R. arrived twenty minutes later, having heard the news while at Wing. She extended her hand to Sutton. "Captain, congratulations. Some airmanship up there today, really some astonishing airmanship. Everyone at Wing was impressed." She stood board-straight shaking Sutton's hand, staring into his bright brown eyes. Shaking his hand, T.R. realized something, something that had begun when she first met Sutton—she admired him.

Sutton took his hand away. The shake was embarrassingly long, and he needed his hand for drinking. Booze had never attracted him, but tonight he was going to get washed. He didn't ordinarily drink this much. Tonight would be a drunk of release, not celebration. There was really nothing to celebrate—he'd merely done his job. When the war was over and they'd won they could cheer and celebrate. He thanked T.R. for her comments.

A few moments later, T.R. sat next to the silent Roger Griffin, sullen because he wasn't part of the limelight. While the others talked, T.R. leaned over and whispered to Griffin: "Buster boy, you can buy me all the booze and beer you want. You can sweet talk me to death, and you can dance me until my feet fall off and buy me all the roses in the world. But I'm telling you this—if you try to lay another hand on this body of mine, I'll bust you right in the chops. Do I make myself clear?"

Griffin screwed up the corner of his mouth.

Toward midnight, Sutton stood and asked Colonel Parker if he could speak with him. "I'd like to know," Sutton asked, "when this top-secret mission is going to happen?"

"Any day now, any day."

Four days later the Chief and Kid Kiley were screaming.

Their yells were simultaneous—two battle klaxons alerting *The Beast's* crew; they were under attack again.

Sutton's squadron had just come off the

target, Antwerp, and were the last squadron in the Group—a formation of one hundred bombers.

The Germans had punched up through a broken layer of cloud at 15,000 feet and were weaving skillfully through the squadron. They probed the squadron's weaknesses but had refrained from making deadly head-on attacks because it was almost impossible to get through. There were too many bombers in front of Sutton's squadron, and now the Germans were making rear and side passes, occasionally coming from below, taking belly shots. Courageous pilots, years of experience, and numerous missions gave them the skill needed to scatter the squadron, which was one of the worst situations that could happen to a bomber formation.

Sutton looked back and felt *The Beast* shivering from the mechanical hammering of the machine guns.

Then he saw *Spot Remover* get hit.

According to the Group's intelligence officer, Maj. Richard Marks, the *Luftwaffe's* number one B-17 ace, Maj. Georg-Peter Eder, would probably be up attacking them today. Eder's speciality, Marks told them in the briefing, was attacking American bombers head-on. Among *Luftwaffe* pilots this tactic was considered suicidal if it was done repeatedly.

"Eder," said the astute Marks, "is a head-on specialist, and thus flies at a very rapid closure rate. This means that your gunners will have a minimum time for firing, and a maximum chance for missing." Marks remark was obvious but he was a humorous man who liked to toss a few jokes into his briefings, which Parker thought was unnecessary but nevertheless allowed, since Marks seemed to amuse the pilots. "We've learned," Marks continued, "that Eder has already been shot down by our bombers four times. He's highly decorated and respected, and he's been wounded nine times. If pilot's were fish," Marks concluded, "Eder would be one big bad barracuda."

"Hey, boss," Kid Kiley said into the interphone, "*Spot Remover* just got hit."

"I see it, Kid," Sutton replied.

Spot Remover was low, two hundred yards back, the last ship in the squadron's sloppy formation. Two thin smoke trails, slightly darker than exhaust smoke, came from the number one and number two engines. Before the smoke appeared Sutton saw two specks speeding towards the wounded bomber. They came slightly above and to the airplane's port side. A second later, he saw two bright flashes in the engines.

"It doesn't look that bad," Sutton said, trying to mask his worst fears. "He seems to be doing okay but keep your eye on him, Kid."

"You better look again," said the Kid.

176

Sutton didn't want to turn.

"Doesn't look good, boss," Tutone said, watching the smoke grow thicker. It spiraled in thick, quick clouds, a deep dirty black mixture of oil and burning aviation fuel. The props were feathering and the ship surged, gained speed, then haltered.

Kid Kiley said, "He's going to slow down soon and he won't be able to keep up."

"No shit," said Tutone, revolving his turret, keeping his eyes out for more fighters. "Those German flyboys are going to come back and finish him off once he falls out of the range of our guns."

"We can't protect him," Rowe said nervously, "we've got to keep up with the squadron." He squeezed the grips of the Bendix chin-turret and his knuckles turned white. From his position he couldn't see *Spot Remover* but from the sound of the radio chatter he had a clear picture of the crippled bomber. "We've got to keep up with the squadron. We can't—"

"Shut up, Rowe!" shouted Sutton. He knew that it was an unwritten Parker law that no ship would side up with a straggler. Although it made sense, it never sat right with the pilots. *If it were me,* most of them thought, *I'd want someone to fall back and give me protection until I got things sorted out.*

Parker wasn't flying today but Chrisp—in command of the squadron—would report every error, every fault made during the mission. He'd already been informed about *Spot Remover* and instructed the pilots to maintain formation.

The smoke streams coming from the engines were briefly interrupted. Once the methyl bromide had been expended from the cylinders through the perforated tubing, the fire began again and the smoke reappeared, thick and deadly.

"I know what you're thinking," Griffin said to Sutton, "and you'd better think again."

"Captain," Kiley said through the interphone, *"Spot Remover's* falling back."

"I can see that, Kid, I can see that."

"What are you going to do, boss?" asked Tutone.

Griffin said. "If you break formation Chrisp will report you and you know Parker'll probably court-martial you."

"Everybody shut up!"

If they continued with the squadron, *Spot Remover* would struggle behind and probably be shot down. The Germans were lurking behind a long thick cloud, waiting like sharks. If Sutton dropped back and gave protection perhaps he could protect the *Fortress* until they flew beyond the fighter's range.

"He's losing more speed," Kiley said.

Something told Sutton to bring back the throttles and fall in alongside *Spot Remover;*

and there was something that told him to forget it. *Think of yourself, the crew, about Chrisp and Parker; keep flying; play it safe.*

"We're going to drop out and help *Spot Remover,*" Sutton said. He drew the throttles back, and *The Beast* lost airspeed and settled lower. Through the windscreen Sutton watched the stacked ships move farther and farther ahead.

"I really don't think this is such a swell idea," said Griffin.

"Keep your eyes on the instruments and look for fighters."

Sutton's earphones cracked with a new voice. "Captain Sutton, this is Captain Chrisp. Get back into formation. Do you copy?"

The Beast was back a hundred yards.

"Captain Sutton, this is Captain Chrisp—I am giving you a direct order to—"

"Here they come!" Bush shouted.

Eder and his wingman were one thousand yards out and one hundred feet above *Spot Remover's* port wing and closing rapidly. Both pilots saw *The Beast* as it pulled along the ship's starboard flank.

"Wilhelm," Eder said, "when I yell 'break,' cut right and dive."

"Jawohl," came the quick reply.

They depressed their trigger buttons. A sparkle of flame came from the bombers' guns, the white tracer rounds streaming past the canopies of the German fighter planes.

"Captain Sutton you are disobeying a direct order! I am ordering you to—"

"Oh, fuck off!"

Eder's aim was precise. He and his wingman, without planning it, had divided *Spot Remover* in half. Eder's strikes hit from the midsection aft, and the wingman's from the midsection forward. Strikes were marked by puffs of smoke and spark. Small chunks of metal fairing flew from the nacelles of the smoking engines. Four hits impacted just below the cockpit, on the pilot's side. One of these, an HE round, exploded when it smashed into the pilot's seat. The concussion killed him instantly and severely wounded the copilot. At six hundred yards they pressed their attack. Smoke streams from their guns marked their path. Two HE rounds struck the number two engine fuel line; a small bright flash erupted. One second later an HE shell from the wingman's fighter crashed through the elevator hinge bracket on the tail with such force that it partially severed the rear gunner's skull and blew out the glass panels of his compartment. Of the forty-six rounds that struck *Spot Remover*, two were most effective. Many had ricocheted off the metal panels and engines or penetrated the fuselage harmlessly.

The copilot felt his bladder and bowels relax; he fell over and whispered two simple words to himself: "I can't."

Of the two effective rounds, one was HE, the other incendiary; they both ignited the feeder and fuel tank in the port wing. The force of the explosion was so terrific that it formed a bisection at the point where the manufacturer at Burbank had joined the wing to the fuselage. Earlier, when the fighters had begun their attack, the turret gunner felt something strike him like a bee sting and looked below; his left foot was missing, chopped by a piece of burning metal spar that had penetrated the fuselage. The sight caused him to gag. Then he screamed.

Spot Remover nosed over. The wing snapped like a bread stick.

"Break!"

The explosion, a huge red-orange fire blossom, momentarily obscured *Spot Remover* and filled the sky with jagged pieces of burned fuselage. The concussive force blew the bombardier through the nose bubble. When it splintered, the acrylic plastic sliced his body like an animal passing through a chain saw. Blackened secions—aerilons, cabling, hoses, braces—fluttered down like feathers from a shotgunned bird. Three and a half minutes later, the turret gunner, disbelieving his footless leg, hit the earth at 120 MPH, still strapped to his seat. To him the descent seemed like three and a half weeks.

"They're all gone," someone said softly on *The Beast's* interphone.

CHAPTER TWELVE

The *Spitfire* flew north at 200 MPH.

It skimmed treetops and slipped over German villages and farmhouses. Sunlight, spilling through large scattered rainclouds, threw sapphire highlights off the polished canopy and glinted white on the wet grassland. The propeller spun silver, a huge pinwheel, and then gray when the cloud shaded the sun. Sharp gold light muted the fighter's colors; but when the sun momentarily vanished behind dark clouds, the colors struck true and showed the black *Balkenkreuz* markings above and below the fighter's blade-like wings.

For six minutes Baerenfaenger skidded the Spitfire around a tall fat column of rain. The maneuver consumed more fuel than planned, and now this worried him because he had only nine minutes of fuel remaining and approximately twelve minutes of flying time before he reached Templehof airfield. It was humid and the sun's rays magnified through the bubble-type canopy. He began to sweat again.

The countryside rolled gently, spilling into all points of the horizon, dotted by trees and sliced by dirt roads and short hills. Baerenfaenger reached down and brought up a handkerchief from a leg pocket and patted his wet face, then he replaced the handkerchief with a battered pair of Zeiss binoculars and scanned the ground.

He searched for two things: *Luftwaffe* flak positions, and the small city of Werder, which was southeast of Berlin on the Havel River. After passing Werder, three minutes later and at a groundspeed of 200 MPH, Templehof would appear. When he spotted Werder he was to make radio contact with the airfield, unless of course he was accidentally brought down by an uninformed *Luftwaffe* flak gun.

He checked his watch: 1550 hours.

At five-five, Baerenfaenger had a boyish appearance, and was one of the shortest pilots in the *Luftwaffe*. A muscular athlete, he performed well both in soccer and on the polo field. He was courageous and fearless. When he engaged in aerial combat, it was these attributes that led him toward his eighty eight victories and ultimate German stardom. Once, after being shot down over France, he was asked by a German reporter what worried him most during his parachute descent onto French soil. "Nothing, really," was his reply. "Surely even the French have heard of me." A quiet, pensive, and moody individual, the Bearcatcher was a man other officers admired. His only true fear, he had confided to a friend, was being trapped in his cockpit, particularly at low altitude. Nothing else bothered him. He'd been shot at by fighters and had received the Black Wound Badge; had been machine gunned by ground troops; and had accidentally flown through telephone wires during a strafing run when he refused to climb away from the target.

Now, his leather flying gloves had turned dark from perspiration, and he used the handkerchief on his face again.

Something appeared ahead. Was it Werder? Or low scrubs and trees? He dipped the left wing and rolled the Zeiss's focus screw. Through the bounce and vibration on the binocular's prisms, Werder came into sharp focus. He worked the fighter's controls and the city rested on the spinner. He depressed the mike button and spoke two words: "Eagle Two."

No response.

He made preparations to land. He placed the glasses back into the case, made one last wipe with the handkerchief, then tightened his shoulder straps and brought the seat up two notches.

"Eagle Two, Eagle Two."

The headset hissed with radio static.

Finally the headset snapped and a clear voice said, "Eagle Two, this is Father Eagle." This was the correct code, and Baerenfaenger was certain now that he would be allowed to land the English *Spitfire* without opposition.

Twenty seconds later he brought the fighter up to three hundred feet. The airport came into view. A row of ten Fw-190s lined a hardstand in front of a hangar. He saw a thin group of figures standing near the fighters.

Now the fuel gauge showed empty, but Baerenfaenger was once again tempted. He had decided. Conceit had won over prudence.

He lined the *Spit*'s nose with the center of the runway. The thin group of figures resolved into more than two dozen officers and men who'd been waiting for him to land. Surely, he thought, one of General-feldmarschall Sperrle's adjutants as well as members of the military and civilian press would be down there; and no doubt there would be photographers. Therefore, he concluded, a moment of Baerenfaenger showmanship was called for in celebration of his momentous victory at Bassingbourn six days ago. It would be a sign for them and they would be expecting it.

At three hundred feet he kicked the fighter's controls and executed a perfect barrel role. The *Spitfire* revolved around its own axis as it piped down the entire length of the runway, the engine roaring under full throttle. He let out another piercing whoop that penetrated the scream of engine noise, then he brought the ship around in a steep left-hand bank.

He loved flying more than anything. More than his soccer victories. More than downing his first British fighter. More than the eighty eight victories and the Knight's Cross that dangled around his neck. Others had done those things, but no one had done what he did at Bassingbourn.

On final approach he glanced down at the crowd. They had applauded when he zoomed through the barrel role, and he could see them cheering wildly.

He approached the end of the runway and the Rolls-Royce Merlin engine ceased sucking fuel; it went dead. The prop jerked to a halt.

The crowd went stiff, momentarily numbed, as if caught by a camera's shutter, not knowing that the Major, Knight's Cross winner, holder of the Black Wound Badge, Bassingbourn victor, and beloved hero of the Third Reich, had the situation in the palm of his sweaty glove. This was a snap. If he planned it, it couldn't have been more spectacular.

With the wheels down and locked and the fighter lined up for a landing, the Bear-catcher glided down to a neat dead-stick landing—a pilot's dream. A beauty—as if planned for a Sunday afternoon airshow crowd. They applauded again, thrilled with this last-minute flourish.

There was enough momentum left in the ship to steer it within twenty yards of the excited crowd. Almost all of the field's *Luftwaffe* personnel had gathered there, and now they were waiting for him to jump out of the cockpit. As he slid the canopy back the *Spitfire* was immediately surrounded.

The photographers jostled their way toward the fighter and took pictures as Baerenfaenger removed his light-weight summer flying helmet and tossed it into the hands of a mechanic. He brushed back his shiny chestnut-colored hair. Someone waved a magnum of *Moet et Chandon* champagne and a bouquet of lilies above the crowd, trying to get his attention. He unclipped his shoulder harness and threw the straps over the back of the seat. Then, grasping the canopy rails, he pushed himself up and stood on the seat and waved.

Flash bulbs popped. Through their glare, on the periphery of the crowd, Baerenfaenger saw the unmistakable collar patch and shoulder-strap insignia of a *Luftwaffe Generaloberst*—a colonel general.

As of 1 March 1935, by a previous Hitler decree, the *Luftwaffe* was to get its own distinctive uniform. The national emblem worn by the other services—the rigid eagle clutching a wreath of oak leaves bearing the swastika—was to be altered. The *Luftwaffe's* version would have a flowing, airy shape, signifying an eagle in flight. The four-pocket hand-sewn service tunic—which the *Generaloberst* wore—was a blue-gray material with matt-aluminum buttons and was tapered at the waist. The collar patches were most distinctive—on a base of square white cloth, the patch contained a gold-bullioned *Luftwaffe* eagle superimposed on a gold wreath of oak leaves. The eagle's outstretched wings were slightly extended over the gold-piped border of the patch. The shoulder straps were a combination of gold and aluminum interwoven on a base of white cloth. Atop this were three, four-sided matt-aluminum pips set in a triangular pattern.

Baerenfaenger thrust his fist into the air. *"Horrido!"* he shouted, then climbed over the cockpit rail and stood on the wing and accepted the *Moet* and the lillies.

More flash bulbs and laughter. More poses and handshakes. The Bearcatcher was enjoying this. He sensed that the *Generaloberst* had come here with word concerning a decoration. The general's small group included his chauffeur and adjutant and a *Luftwaffe* Major and Hauptmann. From where he stood, it was easy to recognize the faces of the young officers:

Maj. Helmuth Hund, the 25-year-old *Kommodore* of *Jagdgescgwader Richthofen II;* and his adjutant, the 26-year-old Hauptmann Prince Ritter von Woll. Baerenfaenger knew them well; they were old friends.

Hund, with twenty six victories and the holder of the Swords and Oakleaves to the Knight's Cross, was the youngest Major in the German Armed Forces—a star among the German people. He was one of three Battle of Britain pilots who received the Oakleaves for gallantry, an award that only went to men with forty or more victories. A dark-haired, handsome man, Hund caused heads to snap when he walked in crowds.

The aristocratic von Woll, with twenty two victories, came from a wealthy Prussian banking family with roots stemming from the fourteenth century. He held the Knight's Cross, the Gold War Order of the German Cross, and the Gold Wound Badge. Four of his wounds were received on separate occasions when he bailed out of burning fighters. A reporter from the magazine *Der Adler* once jokingly wrote that, "with the amount of money expended on *Hauptmann* von Woll's awards and destroyed aircraft, a whole regiment could be outfitted for a major battle." Half-boy, half-idol, his pretty face, rosy cheeks and swept-back golden hair and blue eyes drew glances everywhere. Regardless of age or marital status, Woll would approach any woman who appealed to him, and was equally successful in bed.

Hund, Baerenfaenger, and Woll were in a very elite group of fighter pilots—the exclusive club of Knight's Cross holders.

By written order, the *Ritterkreuze* was worn around the collar, where it dangled conspiciously over the wearer's tie knot—thus the nickname, the "tin tie." The recipient was granted the same respect and awe as movie stars and sports heroes, which was exactly what it was intended to do. Women sought them out; autographs were requested; maitre d's quickly ushered them to choice tables, thankful they had selected their restaurants. Their photographs and stories were in numerous magazines and newspapers. Officers of higher rank would defer to them, while some said that the award was handed out like so many candy bars.

Hund, Baerenfaenger, and Woll were Goering's favorites and had been present at state dinners and receptions at the *Reichmarshal's* palatial home, *Karinhall*. Because of the trio's accomplishments, their stardom, Goering had long ago granted them permission to decorate their fighters with a distinctive, highly visible marking: the entire cowling of each plane was painted flat black, the only such marking in the *Luftwaffe*.

Collectively they were known as the Black Eagles.

They had flown together in the same *Jagdeschwader*—the famous *Richthofen II*—for over two years. Since Baerenfaenger had been on detached duty, today was the first time they'd been together in six months.

Because of Baerenfaenger's hoped-for successful mission and Goering's desire to heavily publicize Sperrle's *Luftflotte II*, an officer with the rank of colonel general had been dispatched with congratulations. "An officer," Goering had said, "with the rank of *Generaloberst* will lend the import needed to greatly publicize the certain success of the Bassingbourn raid." His choice was the ubiquitous Kurt Stahl, a member of the *Luftwaffe's* general staff, an old Goering friend, and holder of the *Pour lé Merite*, the famous "Blue Max," which he'd received in World War I. Stahl was essentially Goering's hatchet man. When least expected, he would appear and disappear at various airfields and outposts, banishing delinquent or remiss officers, promoting and praising others. Today, the *Generaloberst* had brought Baerenfaenger both good and bad news.

After a round of razor-sharp salutes and handshakes with Stahl, Baerenfaenger spent a few light moments discussing old times with Hund and Woll, who then excused themselves from the group.

"First," Stahl said to Baerenfaenger as they drove toward the hangar, "The *Reichmarshal* wishes me to convey his deep appreciation and congratulations. He said that he felt in his heart that the mission would indeed be a success."

Stahl's black Opel slipped to a halt and his chauffeur opened the car door.

"You know," Stahl said, walking into an office in the hangar, "that the *Fuhrer* has been keeping an eye on your progress during this mission."

Surprised, Baerenfaenger said, "I was unaware of that, *Generaloberst*."

"*Ja*. Ever since the plan was conceived and right up to this minute. He's been receiving daily reports from Sperrle's headquarters. The success of this mission means a lot to the *Fuhrer*."

"That is very exciting to hear."

Stahl removed his peaked cap and placed it gently on the office desk.

"*Generaloberst*," Baerenfaenger said, standing at rigid attention, "I think it is a further honor to have someone of your rank here today."

Stahl, a tall slim man with square features, was surprisingly young looking for a 50-year-old general. He was leaning on the desk's edge, his arms folded across his bemedaled chest. He reached up to his throat and touched his *Pour le Merite*. "Goering and I received these together during the First World War. We flew with Richthofen. Some say I got these"—he touched his collar patch insignia—"simply because of that relationship. There's a lot of dislike for me in the Air Force." He spit the word out and reached into a pocket for a cigarette case and offered one to Baerenfaenger. "Please, take one and relax. Have a seat."

Baerenfeanger accepted a light from Stahl's gold Dunhill lighter and sat near the desk, taking a long draw on the cigarette. Something more than he anticipated was in the air. Stahl hadn't come here merely to bring word of further decoration; there was something else. He felt anxious and wished the man would get to the point; but he knew his place, knew that you didn't rush an emissary of Goering's.

Stahl walked around the desk to the window and stood silently for a while. "I've come here for several reasons," he said, turning and facing Baerenfaenger. "First,"—he said with a smile, "to tell you that you have been awarded the Diamonds. I extend to you my congratulations."

Baerenfaenger was stunned. He couldn't believe what he just heard. He expected something, perhaps a promotion, maybe a decoration. But not the Diamonds, Germany's highest award bestowed on the recipient by Hitler himself. When he brought his cigarette up to his lips his fingers were trembling.

"Of course you know the importance of this decoration," said Stahl.

"Jawohl, Herr Generaloberst, I do. I do indeed, and I am very grateful."

There were four levels of Knight's Cross: the Knight's Cross to the Iron Cross, which was instituted on 1 September 1939; the Knight's Cross to the Iron Cross with Oakleaves; the Knight's Cross to the Iron Cross with Oakleaves and Swords; and the Knight's Cross to the Iron Cross with Oakleaves, Swords, and Diamonds. The Diamonds were instituted by Hitler on 15 July 1941 and awarded the next day to the first recipient, *Luftwaffe* ace Werner Molders. The Diamonds were never worn by an enlisted man, nor given to a foreign national—unlike the Oakleaves and Swords, which was given to Japanese Grand Admiral Yamamoto by Hitler in 1943. The Diamonds were imbedded in the pear-shaped Oakleaves award which was above the Swords and the Knight's Cross. Additionally, the hilts of the crossed Swords bore a grouping of diamonds.

Stahl took a seat behind the desk and flicked an ash into an ashtray cut from an

88mm shell casing. "The award," he said, looking into Baerenfaenger's sparkling eyes, "will be presented by the *Fuhrer* in the Reich Chancellery tomorrow. The ceremony is not very long, but it will be memorable. A reception will follow. Goering will be present, along with Sperrle. Hotel accommodations have been reserved for you—a suite in your name at the Adlon Hotel on the *Unter den Linden*. Also present will be your two comrades, Major Hund and *Hauptmann* Woll."

"I am very excited, *Mein Generaloberst.*"

"Yes, I would be, too," Stahl said, crushing his cigarette. He took his eyes off Baerenfaenger and sat back in the desk chair. "Now comes the sour part of my mission." His smile vanished and his face went stiff. "Goering and the *Fuhrer* both concur that you would be more valuable to the Fatherland and the war effort as a living hero rather than a dead one. So orders have been issued, effective today, taking you off combat flying status until further notice."

Baerenfaenger was shocked; his mouth opened and he said, "I . . . I really don't understand, *Generaloberst.*" The sparkle was gone from his face.

"I know this is sad news for you, but you should take consolation in the fact that you have had a very illustrious career at a very young age. You've done things no other flier has done. Bassingbourn was a heroic and courageous act, one that will be written in the history books. And, you've won the Diamonds—the highest decoration Germany can bestow on a soldier."

"But, sir, flying is my blood, my life. It is all I have lived for. I envision giving more to Germany from the air than from behind a podium or collecting money for—"

Stahl raised his hand. "Enough. I understand, Baerenfaenger. You forget, I was a pilot, too. My blood is part gasoline, so I understand these things. I really do. However, the matter is beyond my control. Nothing can be done but to accept your orders and obey, and hope that you will be alive to fly again in the future. You must understand that the *Fuhrer* has made his decision. It is irrevocable. Furthermore"—he placed his hands flat on the desk blotter—"there is something else, in addition to what I have already said."

An ash fell from Baerenfaenger's cigarette and he swept it from his thigh. This was a bittersweet moment, he thought. Everyone pays for what they receive, and he wasn't getting the Diamonds for nothing; it would cost him dearly. He leaned toward the ashtray and stubbed his cigarette. "And what is that, *Generaloberst?*" he asked, the obedient soldier waiting for orders.

"After the award ceremony tomorrow you will be flying escort for Generalfeldmarschall

Sperrle—that is, you, Major Hund and *Hauptmann* Woll. You will depart here from Templehof at 1520 hours and fly guard escort back to Paris. This is a security rating of Top Secret. Once in Paris, the general will present you and the Eagles to various dignitaries. Only after you have arrived in Paris will the flight be given exposure in the press. Do you understand everything I've said, Major?"

"*Jawohl, Mein Generaloberst.*"

"Good."

Stahl stood and put on his peaked cap and came quickly around the desk. Baerenfaenger sprang from the chair. Stahl reached for his hand and shook it with force and placed his other hand on Baerenfaenger's shoulder.

"August," he said, "listen to a fellow aviator—an old bird that has somehow managed to slip by the vultures this long. I know where your heart is. I know that right now you are low because you have been taken off combat flying. Perhaps flying means more to you than the Diamonds. I don't know. But remember this—there is a time for everything; and also remember that many men die too late, and a few too soon. But very few learn the real lesson—and that is to die at the right time. Keep those words locked in your heart when the *Fuhrer* hands you the Diamonds."

Stahl walked to the door. Before he reached for the knob, he stopped, then turned sharply. He faced Baerenfaenger and stood at the position of attention and drew his hand up to his peaked cap. He said: "I salute you August Baerenfaenger." He clicked his heels.

"And I salute you, *Herr Generaloberst.*"

As Stahl went for the door, he said softly, *"Horrido."*

CHAPTER THIRTEEN

Arianne, watching Jim Sutton's brown eyes, poured two high Scotches without ice. She knelt on the floor beside the coffee table to drink.

A ragged moon hung in the night sky and a ray struck through the leaded windows, sparking her cold blue eyes. It was very quiet, and when she moved Sutton could hear the fabric of her clothes brushing her smooth skin. Once he looked at her for a brief moment, not longer, because he had a secret and he did not wish to give it away. Not here, not now.

Her eyes were shadowed, half-hidden by the dark light, and they said so much and yet so little. In them was a beauty that beckoned inquisition, desire that summoned challenge, warmth that mirrored her intelligence. Arianne's mouth was firm, the slim sensitive lips partially parted, as if yearning to speak something he wished desperately to hear—perhaps a secret as deep as his that would never be divulged. Perhaps it was too late to divulge secrets.

Her hands rested motionless on her flannel skirt, the long delicate fingers fluttering nervously only once.

Arianne sipped Scotch and then she asked, "What does it feel like to kill someone?"

"Disappointing."

"Not the thrill you expected?"

"I'm not in this for thrills."

"But I'm trying," Arianne said, brushing her hair back over her shoulder, "to imagine what it's like up there after you kill someone."

"It's a feeling of detachment," Sutton answered, his eyes closed. "You're up there in the sky and the sky is beautiful, and the clouds are beautiful. Everything seems so peaceful, so goddamned deceptively peaceful. And suddenly there are crazy little airplanes coming at you firing their crazy little guns, and even then you can't sense that someone, a faceless human who doesn't even know you, is trying to kill you. And then there's the flak, innocent-looking except that the sky is filled with thousands of unseen steel shreds flying at you at incredible speeds. Sometimes they hit the ship's skin, sounding like hail slamming against a cheap tin wall. Then there's the sound of your own guns firing like jackhammers, shaking the plane until you swear it was going to tear apart. And during all this the crew is bitching about something that's malfunctioning. And while you're flying along you have to be careful that you don't smash into one of your own bombers. It's maddening, absolutely maddening." Sutton picked up his crystal glass and drank some Scotch, then he put it down on the silver coaster, sat up and said, "But it's deceptive, you see, because . . . because it's easy to love it. Because it's so—"

"Exciting?"

He nodded yes then slumped back into the couch, disgusted at the sound of the word.

Before, for a while, they had talked about London in the spring, when the buds popped open like pink badges and the birds sung with joy. They spoke about the sparkle of New York City winters, when excitement and life returned after the heat of the dulling summer. And they talked about rowboats on sleepy streams, about autumn visits to the countryside, about days when they might walk on empty beaches and feel the spray sticking to their skin. They spoke about peace, about Christmases without war, about the joy of life. Arianne told Sutton she loved the rain—thunderstorms like the one they had had a few nights ago when they made love the first time. She told Sutton she loved ice-skating on frozen ponds, walking through grassy fields, and sleeping all day on cloudy Sundays. She liked talking like this: it made her wonder and dream, to expect things she loved and cherished. But then she remembered where she was and where he would be tomorrow, and her expectations fell away with chilling suddenness. In this unguarded moment she had almost given up her secret, as if it would brush away her despair. When they stopped talking she poured more Scotch and sat again in silence, wondering if she had revealed too much.

"Excuse me," Arianne said, staring down at the tops of her nervous hands. "I shouldn't have asked you that."

"Asked me what?"

"About your feelings up there . . . about killing."

"I'm sort of glad you did. I mean, I never heard myself say it before. I've thought about it but I've never admitted it."

She lit their cigarettes with a lighter, a gold Dunhill.

It took her a few moments to figure out where she wanted to go with her thoughts and she said something about fear, looking at the silver framed photo of her dead husband, saying something about how he didn't have it and if he did maybe he'd be here complaining about taking the trash out, and that you needed fear because it held you back before you did something stupid *like trying to be a bloody awful hero when you should act like a scared little boy*.

"We all have to pull the sheets over our

heads once in a while. It keeps the demons away," she said, taking his hand.

"There are things everyone finds hard to admit."

"I hope you admit you are afraid about tomorrow," Arianne said, "because the world is made up of fools who never admit to what they are. Perhaps your copilot, Griffin, is like that. They seem to go on deceiving themselves and the people around them who love them. They have nothing to hold them back from the edge of self-inflicted doom."

Sutton could have sat there and looked at the Persian rug or the hard oak walls while he listened to her, but she was using her eyes, and he looked back, at the things they said, at the way she moved her body. She'd only meant to go so far with him, a fast car ride, a sexual release on a rainy night, and then that would have been that. But now she was in over her head and she hadn't expected that. You never do, because you never expect someone to have the same secret and to say it with their eyes at the exact moment you do.

If tonight was a night for divulging secrets, T.R. would be the exception.

She sat alone in a jeep in front of the Officers' Club, and that ragged old moon was working a sadness into her heart that she hadn't felt for a long time. The tempo from the club orchestra hit a bounce and the singer came up stage and knocked out lyrics that brought tears to her eyes, that made her remember him.

"Hey, Shatzi," she had said to him, "how 'bout letting me cut a few turns in the clouds with this bird chaser here." T.R. was referring to Shatzi's airplane.

Shatzi was her man and he was pumping some octane into the home-built Pitts Special with a red paint job that blinded people on sunny days. Shatzi was already a local star—a winner of numerous air races, and a showman capable of fancy aerobatic maneuvers.

When he looked up at her he gave a lopsided grin and put his hands on his hips and said, "T.R., this ain't no chimney flyabout. And besides, you're still an egg."

"Egg, hell. All's I want to do is take it up and lay it on the railroad—you know, low and slow. How 'bout it one time? You told me when we first met that you'd let me haul it up and punch a few holes in the sky."

"I must've been drunk or stupid," Shatzi said, shaking his head.

He was tall and lean, like an elevator cable, and had a strong, sensitive face. When he walked into a place the cookies would turn twice because they thought it could be Clark Gable. He wore one of those Gable mustaches, a thin pencil job, and his shoulders had a rugged slouch, as if he was about to attack someone. TR. was so in love with Shatzi that when she first started dating him she lost ten pounds from not eating or sleeping. "It's the best diet in the world," she told a friend. "He just does crazy things to me, but he's never put a hand on me."

One night at a dance, the band was cutting the same tune she heard now in front of the Officers' Club:

She gets too hungry for dinner at eight;
She loves the theatre but never comes
late;
She never bothers with neurotics she
hates;
That is why the lady is a tramp.

"That song is you, T.R.," Shatzi whispered in her ear while they danced. T.R. giggled and then Shatzi picked up a line, tailored it, and sang it off-key in her ear. "You love the fresh wind in your hair, life without care, hates parties and dresses, just loves flying all day . . ."

Two weeks later Shatzi was up in the Pitts, doing a few rolls and loops, when the left wing snapped off like a stale bone. A few hours after the fire burned out a search party found a couple of pieces of Shatzi spread across the side of a mountain.

Now, T.R. heard someone and when she turned she saw Roger Griffin walking up to the jeep. She shoved her hand in her pocket and searched for a Kleenex.

"Hey, T.R.," Griffin said, draping his arm over the jeep's windshield. "how 'bout a beer or something? Say, are those tears in your eyes?"

"No, they're raindrops," T.R. said, wiping her eyes.

"But it's not raining."

"And these aren't teardrops either, hot-shot."

"Hey, look, T.R., I just saw you sitting here in the dark alone and thought you might want to have a beer or something. Also, I want to apologize for what happened in Parker's room the other night."

"Apology accepted."

"Good. Now that that's out of the way, how 'bout a beer or something?"

"I gotta go. I have a big day tomorrow, and from what I hear, so do you."

"Come on, give a guy a break. I'll give you an intimate description of my famous loop."

"Roger, you know something, you seem to have this belief that everyone that meets you thinks you're the greatest. I guess that's the way you were brought up—thinking that you were the world's greatest, on the ground and in the air. Well, I'm here to tell you that you're not. Okay? Now, excuse me," T.R. said, reaching for the ignition.

"Wait a second," Griffin said, putting his hand on the steering wheel. "Now I get it. You're sitting out here crying over someone—a guy, that's what. Some guy that bounced you, right?"

"That's none of your damned business."

"I wouldn't be surprised if it was Jim Sutton, everybody's brown-eyed hero."

T.R. lifted Griffin's hand off the wheel and started the engine. "One of these days," she said, "someone should drop an airplane on your big fat head. Maybe that'd cut it down to size."

"I saw the way you looked at Sutton when we came back from Brest. You're in love with the guy, that's what," Griffin said.

"You astonish me, you really do. You think you're so terrific you can just elbow your way into people's lives, don't you?"

"Hey, look, I'm just calling a spade a spade, is all."

T.R. put the clutch in, shifted into reverse. "Despite everything, Rog, I'd like to wish you all the luck in the world tomorrow. I hope you and the guys come back. In the meantime, I'd like to tell you a few things: First, what I feel and how I feel toward anyone is my business, not yours; second, I don't appreciate you nosing around me. I just want to be friends with you, Roger, that's all. Good night."

When she pulled the jeep away from the Officers' Club, T.R. heard the last line from the song:

Hates California, it's corny and damp
That's why the lady is a tramp.

CHAPTER FOURTEEN

Colonel Parker was sitting behind his desk with his arms folded. His stomach felt sour and his face was drawn tight with tension. His eyes were fire-bright; they glowed coal-hot with anger. The blood had escaped his head and turned his features ash-gray.

The office was quiet.

For the past thirty seconds Sutton had been standing at attention, ordered that way by Parker and told not to offer any comments unless asked a direct question.

"There are two folders on my blotter, Captain Sutton," Parker said. "The plain folder is a report of today's action in which you disobeyed a direct order; it was written up by Captain Chrisp. The other folder"—he tapped it—"with the red band was brought down here a while ago by Major Marks and Colonel Hayme, the intelligence officer from Wing."

Sutton smiled. "You're not entertaining the idea of court-martialing me, are you,

Colonel? Because, if you are, you can find another boy for your secret mission, which I assume is in that folder." He pointed to the red band resting under Parker's skinny hand.

"You disobeyed a direct order, Captain," said Parker, folding his arms.

"You can accuse me of a lot of things, but you'll never accuse me of being a fool. You don't think I'd take the mission under threat of a court-martial, do you?"

Parker thought for a few seconds, then he said: "No, I suppose not." He moved the Chrisp folder away toward the side of the desk. "But," he added. "I'm obliged to keep it here," knowing he'd made the right decision because there was too much riding on the secret mission: career, advancement, a chance to be included in the Air Force's history books. And he was certain, too, that he hated Sutton because Sutton had painted him into a corner. He needed Sutton; Sutton was the only pilot capable of flying the mission; without him, his career would come to a halt right here in his office.

"Just ask yourself this," Sutton said, standing easier, "how would it look if you court-martialed the pilot you've chosen to fly your secret mission?"

What could Parker say? He knew Sutton was right. "Okay," he said. "If you take the mission I'll forget about this." He placed his hand on the Chrisp folder.

"I want to fly this mission, Colonel, I really do. It's a challenge. And I'm sure *The Beast's* crew would want to fly it as soon as they hear about it. There's a bunch of loony guys in that crew but they can handle anything you or the Germans hand them.

"All right," Parker said. He made a noise like gas escaping from an inflated balloon.

Sutton picked up the red-banded folder and read the paragraph on the cover:

TOP SECRET

This document contains information affecting the national defense of the United States within the meaning of the Espionage Act, 50 U.S.C. 31 & 32, as amended. Its transmission, or the revelation of its contents in any manner to an unauthorized person or persons, is prohibited by law.

Sutton opened the folder and read a covering memorandum:

TO: 8th Air Force Commander

The attached radio transmission was intercepted at 1230 hours on 1 May 1944. It was originated by the *Oberkommando der Luftwaffe* (German Air Force High Command), Berlin, and was transmitted to General Sperrle, Commander, *Luftflotte III*, headquartered in Paris, France:

"The Fuhrer requests that you be present at the New Reich Chancellery at 1200 hours on 7 May 1944, when the Fuhrer will present the Diamonds award to Maj. August Baerenfaenger. Per your request, the Fuhrer has granted you permission to have Major Baerenfaenger escort you back to your headquarters for approximately two weeks detached duty. Accompanying the Major, and acting as additional fighter escort, will be Major Hund and Hauptmann Woll. Departure from Templehof Airfield will be at 1500 hours.

It should be noted that Baerenfaenger, Hund, and Woll are three of Germany's top aces, and are highly decorated and revered by the German people. Collectively, they are known as "The Black Eagles," and are continually given wide coverage in the German press. It is the opinion of this office that their elimination would be psychologically negative, not only to the *Luftwaffe,* but the people of Germany

The following recommendations would seem both propitious and suited to accomplishing this goal:

(1) To intercept the Sperrle aircraft over France
(2) To eliminate Sperrle, Baeren-faenger, Hund, and Woll
(3) To utilize the flying skill of a singular aircraft with sufficient firepower, range, etc.—i.e., the B-17

It is the feeling of this office that a singular attack by one B-17 would not arouse the suspicion of the mission's objective; whereas, the presence of a heavy fighter force might be relayed and possibly understood as an intention to intercept Sperrle. Therefore, we feel a low-level mission by a B-17 flown at ground level to the point of interception would be successful. It is the recommendation of this office that a pilot possessing low-level flying skills, as well as the experience necessary be utilized as the command pilot.

Sutton folded the page over and his eyes darted over the top of the folder for a moment. Unlike Parker, he was relaxed now.

"Please keep reading," Parker said.

The remainder of the report contained photos and biographies of the Black Eagles. There were descriptions of the aircraft they would be flying—Fw-190s. Sperrle would be using his personal *Junkers Ju* 52, recently outfitted with three new BMW engines. Elaborate graphs showed possible altitudes, a description of the terrain the flight would pass over, the type formation they would employ. A thorough description of the Junker's command pilot was furnished along with the achievements of the three fighter pilots, lastly noting that it was Baerenfaenger who'd flown over Bassingbourn. It was for this mission, the report stated, that he was being awarded the Diamonds. In summation, the report stated that the combined force of three aces would be formidable opponents against any attacking B-17 and should not be dismissed as easy prey. Several color photographs were furnished showing the distinctive black cowl insignia of the Fw-190s.

Sutton closed the folder and Parker said, "Baerenfaenger is the bastard who shot this place up a few days ago. Make sure you shoot that sucker down first." There was anger in his voice. "As you can see, I couldn't tell you anything specific the day you came on board because the plan was still being formulated and needed final approval all the way to the top."

Parker knew that no other pilot had Sutton's qualifications. Sutton began flying at the age of thirteen; his father owned an airstrip, and he'd done crop-dusting during the summer. And, he was an outstanding

B-17 pilot.

The fire simmered in Parker's eyes. They were round again, less glassy. The lids had widened when he watched Sutton enthusiastically flipping through the red-banded folder. "If you complete the mission," Parker stated, "there'll be plenty for you."

"And if the mission isn't successful?"

"Then, Captain, I'll send roses to your girlfriend."

Early that evening, *The Beast's* crew was in Colonel Parker's office, along with Major Marks and Colonel Hayme. Hayme and Marks had spread a large map of France on the conference table. The map contained intersecting lines of blue and red, which Marks had drawn with grease pencils and a ruler. Red indicated the course Sperrle and the Eagles would take after departing Berlin; blue, the line of flight *The Beast* would be on. The two lines intersected over Reims, where, according to the plan, the crew of *The Beast* would destroy the four aircraft.

"All right, listen up," Marks said sharply, tapping his ruler on the map like a college professor. "I don't care how many times you've heard this in the past couple of hours." He had presented the plan to the crew several times, and now he sensed their attention dwindling. But getting them totally interested wasn't his job, that was Parker's responsibility. Marks was here to brief them. He made each of them stand and recite, verbatim, his part of the overall mission.

"The plan is simple," Marks said in a singsong voice, using the ruler for emphasis, slapping it hard on the map. "The Eagles leave Berlin at 1500 hours and join up with the Sperrle aircraft. They will refuel once and take a short rest. Then, they will fly directly to Paris. Their arrival time will be approximately 1600 hours. The Germans, as you know, are a very precise people, so we can count on their punctuality. The Eagle group will then be passing over here." He pointed to Reims on the map. "At approximately 1530 hours. That, gentlemen, is the point of interception. You must place *The Beast* between that point and Paris. Once you actually engage the group, you must pull in as close as possible to Sperrle's aircraft and shoot him down as quickly as you can.

"Why," he asked Sutton, "should you follow this procedure?"

By rote, Sutton said, "The closer we get to the Junkers, the larger the target will be. This will also make it difficult for the Eagles to shoot at us for fear they will hit Sperrle."

"You must," Hayme interrupted, "stay as close as you can. Remember, according to our intelligence sources, Sperrle's aircraft will be flown by a substitute pilot. Sperrle's normal pilot will be on leave. We're hoping he won't be as tenacious or as experienced as the regular pilot."

"Now," Marks asked, "what about the attack approach? Lieutenant Griffin, perhaps you can give us that answer."

"We should attempt to come in from behind and below the group since this is their blind spot. As we approach, we should begin firing on Captain Sutton's order."

"And only his order," Parker added.

There was a flurry of coughs and groans. Tutone smiled. The Chief passed out cigarettes and asked Tutone what he thought. "A snap," he answered boastfully. "We're gonna get us some Germans."

Marks tossed the ruler across the map and continued. "Well, if you miss the first pass, the only thing that's going to be snapping is the lid on your coffin, because you won't get a second chance. It's like putting a bet down on a horse: Once the bell goes off, that's it. You're dealing with aces here, not a bunch of school kids up on their first flying lesson."

"Here! Here!" Bo Baker shouted. "Give 'em hell, Rick." He gave one of his high-pitched laughs and added, "Why don't you come up with us and repeat that speech."

"I would, but losing at the race track is much easier."

Parker had been sitting with his arms folded, listening.

He was moved by the history of the occasion. It was unfolding before his eyes, and he had plans for visiting the Pentagon years from now and going through the files and pulling out everything concerning the mission. As he listened, he made notes on a small pad. He was sending men out on a mission to destroy three of Germany's top aces and one of the *Luftwaffe's* highest ranking officers. This would be a chapter in the book he intended to write — or part of the lectures he would surely give at West Point and other universities after he retired. This was a grand occasion — young men preparing to go off on a secret mission, making the ultimate sacrifice. Fantastic, he thought. Maybe a whole book should be written about this.

Marks signaled and Sutton stood. "All right," he asked his men, "any questions?"

The room was silent and they looked at each other for a few moments.

Finally Parker stood. He cleared his throat, moved by the history of the occasion. "Okay, I want you all to get a good night's rest. Also, I just want to say good luck and God's speed. Tomorrow will be an important day in all our lives — especially yours. I want to thank you for what you will be doing."

CHAPTER FIFTEEN

Shortly after high noon, *The Beast's* crew arrived at a special section marked off in the Officers' Mess.

Sutton sat between Griffin and Tutone and had a big Amerian lunch of baked ham, potatoes, green beans, buns, and black coffee. They barely spoke. Parker sat at the head of the table opposite Sutton and appeared more nervous than the men who were going off on this special mission. No one looked at their watches but when Sutton got up and left, the rest sauntered behind and walked to the Operations hut.

Parachutes, escape kits and .45 automatics were handed out. Each man had to sign for five hundred dollars worth of French francs. Tutone was talking about a scheme to keep the money after the mission, saying he was thinking about "losing" it through an open hatch. Kid Kiley told them he'd never seen that much money in his whole life. "By the way," Parker told him as they walked out of the hut a few minutes later, "you're the youngest tail gunner in the Eighth Air Force. We just found out that you turned eighteen last Friday. Happy birthday."

A covered truck pulled up to the hut and sat waiting, the exhaust notes beating out a steady tempo. The crew jumped aboard and slid down cool benches. Rowe banged his fist on the cab and they lurched forward. Tutone lit a cigarette.

The truck was filled with silence. They'd taken this ride together before, going out to their ship—but this was different.

When they reached *The Beast* they jumped from the truck and began hauling their gear through the hatches. Griffin walked under the starboard wing and began talking with Holden.

Now, standing under *The Beast's* nose, Sutton realized how lucky he and the crew were. As disjointed as they'd been in the beginning, their ship, their home, had brought them together.

The Beast which was one of those ships that tells you after its first flight, was all right. Like a good running Ford or Chevvy, or a classy Caddy that purrs to you, assures you that everything is put together correctly. Some B-17s were pure lemons and no matter what was done, everything would go wrong day after day. Flaps wouldn't work, guns would misfire, the landing gear wouldn't lock, valves would fail. Bad planes. A lot of them were just plain duds and a crewman could tell, could smell it a hundred yards away. And no matter how hard the maintenance people worked over their bodies, the damned things would never function properly, so that just climbing into them or looking at them sitting on the tarmac, gave a guy a bad case of the willies. In the air or on the ground, they would shake and moan, beg to be grounded or turned around on a raid, children never wanting to leave home, never really capable of doing what they'd been designed to do. The Chief said these planes had been slapped together on Monday, when the factory people had come off a drunken weekend; either that or on a Friday, "when nobody gives a shit about a rivet or a wire because they have their minds on booze and weekend pussy. Monday and Friday planes are fucked up."

Tutone told Sutton that the Chief had actually spent hours going through the records and found that *The Beast* had been rolled out of the Long Beach, California factory, and that was swell by him because it was a drizzly Wednesday and no one cared too much for being outdoors, and that this meant she was sound. The Chief knew the exact time, the exact date, and all the major inspectors who had reviewed *The Beast's* body.

"It is a humble ship," the Chief told Tutone. "But it is solid," he had declared with a tone of authority."

No one disputed the Chief. No one wanted to. Especially now, before this mission. They needed something extra, and this was it—a belief in their ship. That was why the Chief felt good climbing into her now: he knew when she was made and who made her and the date she was made, and all this information was all right. The crew called this "The Chief Whitefeather Seal of Official Indian Approval." It was their amulet and they would silently wear it, and would always be thankful to him for discovering it. Any evil spirit had been dispelled. The ship had been aired and she was good. And this was the beginning of their belief in themselves and their ability as a cohesive crew.

As Sutton stared at her he knew it had to be more. He knew they needed something to bring them back from this mission. He knew it had to be more than just the airplane. Because he knew that half of the lemons never came back, and that 50 percent of the beauties never came back. So it had to be more. It had to be more than her sleek lines, her neat framework, the heavenly roll-out date the Chief had discovered going through her paperwork, or the words of mechanical confidence from Holden. In his pilot's mind and heart, Sutton knew that it would take more to bring them together like this. And despite this, despite his desire for a transfer after this mission, to leave Parker, he cared.

Holden had found it boring working on *The Beast,* "because there ain't much that has to be done. She's solid," he had said, repeating the Chief's words.

Holden walked away from Sutton and kicked the tire hard, his hands in his back pockets, looking as if he didn't give a damn when everyone knew that he did. "Solid!" He said the word loudly, walking away from her, not glancing back, fearful that he'd give away too much feeling for her. After the crew saw this, after hearing the Chief's verdict, they were perfectly satisfied that their ship was all right.

And thank God for that, because every time they'd board her from then on, they knew that she was a sound airplane.

Sutton had come close to explaining this to Arianne. Only a woman, he felt certain, could appreciate the sensitivity required to relate what he felt—the depth of feeling he had for his ship. Arianne had expressed her understanding the way only a woman could. It was in her eyes, the way she listened to his thoughts about his cherished airplane, the holder of his life.

Now, a car pulled up and two men stepped out, a reporter and a photographer from the Signal Corps. A newsreel camera was set up on a tripod. Sutton eyed them with contempt. Griffin and Holden came over to him.

"Does that thing," Sutton said, jerking his thumb at *The Beast,* "have gas in it?"

Holden said, "Can't squeeze another drop in 'er, Captain. You can go to New York and back, if you like. I'll send you the bill in the morning."

Sutton checked his watch, then a hand grabbed his arm from behind.

"So long, Captain."

Sutton turned. It was Colonel Parker. Cole stood beside him.

"Once again," Parker said, "I'd like to wish you and your men good luck."

Reluctantly, Sutton shook his hand and then Tutone walked up to them and everyone was smiling nervously, not really knowing what to say now.

A small crowd had gathered around Parker and the photographer, who was taking a long shot of the crew as they climbed aboard *The Beast.* "A very nice touch," Sutton said to Parker sarcastically, referring to the cameramen. Then Sutton turned to Holden and thanked him.

"Shit," Holden said, mashing his cigar between his teeth, "she's a good solid bird." Then he shook Sutton's hand and added, "We'll see ya for dinner." They saluted each other.

Griffin followed Sutton through the forward hatch and they strapped in and went through the pre-flight check list. The sun had heated up the cockpit, but they were sweating from nerves. Each item, each switch, valve, was gone over, but with great concentration. Battery switches, mixture control, parking brake, radio frequency, cowls, air filters, control surfaces; they were all checked. Then they went through the engine start procedure.

Field activity had slowed.

Holden and his mechanics were standing by, almost at attention. A cloud had slipped by and the sun broke through and lit up the figure of Doc Matlin, his head peering through the window of an ambulance. T.R. leaned against the front fender, arms folded, a pensive expression on her pretty face. Nearby, a few large fire extinguishers were resting on the grass. Sutton pulled on his harness, making sure the straps were tight. His collar was wet with perspiration.

Holden stood near the nose section and gave the thumbs-up sign when the number one engine coughed to life. A thin wisp of light blue exhaust smoke came from the sputtering cylinders. Holden continued holding his thumb up, and then the engine caught and banged into life. Mechanics dashed around *The Beast* now, pulling away chocks from the wheels. Doc Matlin stepped out of the ambulance and closed the door.

The number two engine caught, and a ferocious roar stabbed the air. The ship vibrated, eager to leave. Sutton stuck his head through the window and took a glance at the running engines, then he directed Griffin to start engine number three. Holden signaled thumbs-up again and watched engine number four's propeller slice the air. Sutton looked away from the engines. He saw T.R. She made a motion with her hand—a quick wave. But for who? All of them? Griffin?

Sutton turned to Griffin and said, "She came down to see you off."

"No, she didn't," Griffin said. "That's for you."

Holden signaled, and Griffin released the parking brake located on his side of the cockpit. A few cars pulled up, various personnel spilled out. Hayme and Marks were there, holding their caps against the wind. Other men ran from the hangar area and gathered near the taxiway in the distance. *The Beast* lumbered toward the active runway, turned, then sped off into the sky.

CHAPTER SIXTEEN

Maj. August Baerenfaenger walked out of the lobby of the Adlon Hotel on *Unter den Linden* and saw the newspaper headline:

BAERENFAENGER TO RECEIVE DIAMONDS

In his excitement to dress and be down here on time to meet the waiting car the *Luftwaffe* had sent for him, he had neglected to buy a newspaper. He would have to wait until after the ceremony to buy a copy for inclusion in his scrapbook.

A *Lutwaffe Unterfeldwebel* stood beside the opened door of a green Mercedes. When he saw Baerenfaenger he clicked his heels, waited for his salute to be returned, then held the door open. "Good day, *Herr Major*. I am here to drive you to the Reich Chancellery." Baerenfaenger thanked him and slipped into the impressive automobile.

It had all been worth it, he thought, as

they drove toward *Friedrich Strasse*—the sacrifices necessary to learn his skills, the near-death situations he'd been through, the pain he had suffered losing close friends, the moments of fading confidence when he wanted to give up flying. And of course there were the wounds he had endured. He had always pushed himself, extended himself beyond the vision of his own limits. Often, he had felt his heart going like a water pump during the night before a sortie until he thought his blood would burst through the top of his head; he had never told anyone this. He had never told anyone about the sleepless nights when he would get up and go vomit from fear, when his hands wouldn't stop shaking and his skin would turn slimy from perspiration. He'd seen himself die a torturous death, and often wondered what was worse: living this silent horror contained in his mind, in his dreams; or being killed by the enemy up there in the clouds.

The Mercedes headed toward *Voss Strasse* where it would turn right again on *Wilhelmstrasse*. From there it would be a short distance to the Reich Chancellery.

He thought about last night. He had been at a friend's apartment on the fashionable *Kufuerstendamn*, which was in the middle-class borough of Charlottenburg. Hund and Woll had been present. There was wine, champagne, caviar, and attractive, wealthy women. Some had a difficult time restraining their admiration, their awe of the Eagles. Not just looks or glances, but countless little gifts of praise that seemed unending. Baerenfaenger wanted the evening to go on forever; he wanted to bathe in the warm lights of stardom until he was fused into a bronze statue that would stand forever as a reminder of his accomplishments. But that only lasted for a while, and then he wondered—he wondered about his confidence, about the worth of his life, his value as a pilot. On the road to glory, he was sure, one paid for everything one received.

The Mercedes turned on the *Wilhelmstrasse* and slipped to a halt in front of the Reich Chancellery. The driver jumped out and opened the door. At the building's majestic main entrance, a tall, rigid, blond SS officer came out and greeted him cordially. A black-uniformed *Fuhrerbegleitkommando* —an SS honor guard—jerked to attention as they strode into the massive building.

Baerenfaenger felt out of place as he walked down the Long Gallery toward the Cabinet Room where the Diamonds would be presented by Hitler.

There was a harshness to this room, to this building. The floor and door arches were green marble, and huge tapestries hung from the distant ceilings. The place had the scent of expensive cologne and perfume, of polished wood and fresh-cut flowers—sharp contrast to cordite and gasoline. This was a building for the politicians and the generals.

The SS officer led him into a small room. From behind a closed door that led to the Cabinet Room polite laughter punctuated the polite conversation. He wished he were back in the sky.

CHAPTER SEVENTEEN

The land around Bassingbourn spread out. The green of the grass dulled and the wheat fields grew smaller, as they dropped back behind *The Beast*. Trees formed a delicate lacy carpet. A small boy looked up and waved from his bicycle. Kid Kiley waved back, certain the boy couldn't see him.

Gibson checked his watch.

It was 1515 hours.

"Laon."

Gibson announced it with a whisper. It was the last checkpoint before Reims.

At an altitude of less than 100 feet, spotting Laon wasn't easy. He'd been told to watch for two church spires atop a hill. This would be the only landmark at such a low altitude, and computing this with the time traveled and *The Beast's* airspeed he found himself surprised with his accuracy. Looking through the navigator's dome, he confirmed the meteorologist's prediction—stratocumulus clouds between two and three thousand feet; visibility, moderate; winds, from the northwest.

"We'll be approaching Reims in twelve minutes," he announced confidently.

This was a signal for Sutton. "Let's keep a sharp lookout," he announced over the interphone. "We're going up." He increased the power setting by first increasing the mixture controls, pulling back on them; then he pulled up on the four propeller controls at the base of the console above the elevator trim wheel. The last motion was gripping the middle handle on the throttle control, palm upward, and moving it forward. He pulled back on the half-moon-shaped control wheel and *The Beast* rose toward the cloud layer.

Now, Sutton recalled Marks's words: *The Eagles should approach at approximately 5,000 feet, so as soon as you spot Laon you should begin your ascent and start searching the sky for them.*

The Chief stood at his waist position, hands curled around the handles of the .50-caliber machine gun. "See anything?" he shouted at Bush.

"Yeah," Bush replied, "lots of French trees."

Sutton was nervous. This wouldn't be the best altitude to engage three of Germany's top aces.

At 1525 hours, with his .50-calibers pointing forward and parallel with the center-line of *The Beast*, Benny Tutone spotted four black specks through the recticles of his guns.

"Eagles straight ahead!" he squawked.

Sutton and Griffin saw them sweeping through *The Beast's* flight path—four petite insects against a clean wall of blue light.

"Three thousand, maybe four thousand yards ahead at twelve o'clock level," Sutton said, evenly. He gave *The Beast* more throttle and she gathered speed, the engine tone going higher.

Rowe felt his mouth go dry.

Skolinsky felt his groin tighten.

Kid Kiley was mad because he couldn't see the fighters from the tail position. He looked down at the emergency handle on the compartment door for the hundredth time, dreading the thought of being caged back here.

The Chief tensed his jaw muscles and scanned the sky.

Griffin didn't want to be here. The whole damned thing was a crazy idea, a publicity stunt. He'd been involved in publicity stunts and knew when he saw one. They would all die, he was thinking, driven down by three aces from the Third Reich who'd be damned first before they let one lone B-17 knock out a *Generalfeldmarshal*. He was being used, he was sure, because Parker was certain to get more publicity with Griffin as a crewman: FAMOUS AVIATOR ON

234

Keeping his turret trained on them, Tutone said: "They haven't spotted us yet, boss. If they did, they'd be turning into us."

Gibson piped in: "The longer they keep going out like that, the better chance we have of coming up underneath."

The Eagles didn't appear deadly—four innocent ships lumbering along at four thousand feet, flying a strange formation. The Junker's speed was surely holding them back, and the formation was surprisingly loose—Woll, twenty yards off the Junker's left wing; Hund twenty yards off the right. Baerenfaenger was up and behind fifty or sixty yards. It was a ragged diamond formation.

At 1500 yards the Eagles passed over the line of *The Beast's* right wing and Sutton turned into them. He aimed behind their flight path, two hundred yards below. The distance narrowed.

"Don't shoot until I give the signal," he said. "Do you understand that? Tutone?"

"Roger, boss."

"Rowe?"

"Rog."

"Skolinsky, how 'bout you?"

"Yes, sir."

"If we don't fire at the right moment we're dead," Baker blurted out. Sweat covered his face.

The insect shapes grew. Their camouflaged colors resolved as *The Beast* drew closer.

1,000 yards.

Sutton's gloved hands were wet.

Beads of perspiration rivered down Griffin's face and stained his freshly pressed collar. Even the loop wasn't this frightening. At least it was rehearsed. This was deadly.

Tutone took deep breaths, like a swimmer before an important race. He charged his guns, pulled back on each handle twice, then flipped on the gun-selector switches. He set the target dimensions on his sight and adjusted the range knob until the recticles framed the target.

"How far are they?" Kid Kiley asked.

No one replied.

Griffin took a gulp of air and let it out slowly. His hands were shaking and he shook his head with disgust. "Stupid," he said under his breath.

Sutton pressed the interphone button and the right side of the control wheel and paused before speaking.

700 yards.

Then Sutton announced, "In about thirty seconds we'll begin firing. But wait for my command."

Kid Kiley had a desire to relieve himself, something he'd done a half hour ago. The urge seemed uncontrollable. He couldn't understand why; then it hit him: fear.

The Chief squeezed the .50-caliber's

handles and wanted to stick his head through the waist window so he could see the German planes. He hated standing there waiting. It was harder for him to breathe now and he could feel his heart smacking against his chest.

Baerenfaenger glanced down at the Junker's silhouette. Sun winked off the glass windows and burnished the spinning props. He was thinking for the three of them: this was a boring flight with a lackluster destination ahead of them. They would be wined and dined, certainly, but what lay ahead in Paris, aside from some pretty women, would be nothing compared to combat duty. They would be spending their days promoting the *Luftwaffe*, sharing cocktails and dinner with colonel generals and other officers, meeting the troops stationed there, attempting to boost their morale. But flying would be another world, and they would be far removed from its excitement and challenge. Despite its deadly quality, Baerenfaenger felt more at home in the air than behind a crystal cocktail glass dressed in formal, full-dress uniforms. In the air, he was an eagle, on the ground he was a bird with pared wings, out of his element and unsure of himself.

500 yards.

"Ritter," Baerenfaenger said into his

throat mike, "remember that girl at the party last night? The one with the big melons?"

"*Jawohl.*"

"I think she wanted to go to bed with you."

Ritter von Woll laughed. "I think she will."

"What?"

"I got her address. She will be in Paris next week."

Hund pressed his mike button. "At this rate of speed," he said dryly, "we will be in Paris next year."

Woll and Baerenfaenger agreed. If they flew any slower they'd fall asleep, Hund thought. He wondered if any German fighter pilots had died from boredom.

CHAPTER EIGHTEEN

"Keep your eyes on those instruments," Sutton ordered Griffin.

400 yards.

"We can do it now, boss."

"Knock it off, Tutone!"

"We're close enough to fire."

"I said wait for my command."

The fighters lines were distinct now, the cowls flat black. They were hanging loosely around Sperrle's aircraft, bobbing up and down slightly.

"Tutone!" Sutton yelled. "Stop moving the turret back and forth."

"I'm deciding which one to fire at."

"Swivel your head instead," said Rowe.

"I'm keeping the hydraulic fluid warm."

"The hydraulic fluid is warm enough and don't argue with me," Sutton bellowed into the interphone. "I'll tell each one of you who to fire at."

The B-17G had eight guns capable of firing forward: two in the chin turret; one on each side of the navigator's compartment; and the two .50s in the belly turret. Sutton would decide which man would fire at what target.

Now, he underestimated his airspeed. If he didn't bring the power back, at this setting he'd overshoot the formation like a locomotive slamming into a stalled boxcar. He brought the throttles back and asked Griffin: "Airspeed?"

"One-fifty."

He brought them back further.

"Airspeed?" he asked, after a few seconds.

"One-three-five and decreasing. We're going to go under them unless—"

"Shit!" Sutton punched the word out. "Give me five-degree flaps. *Fast!*"

Griffin's left hand shot down to the wing flap switch on the control pedestal and the flaps rolled down.

"Airspeed?"

"One-two-fiver."

The Beast shuddered and vibrated like a boat dragging anchor.

Sutton pressed the interphone button.

"Tutone," he ordered, "you take the fighter above the tail section."

"Roger, boss, the fighter above the Junker's tail."

"Rowe? Are you still breathing down there?"

"Barely."

"Take the fighter on the left wing. Each

of you fire directly under the cockpit, then fire at the Junker's engines. Tutone, you take starboard. Rowe, you take the port. Do you copy?"

"Roger, boss."

"Yo."

"The rest of you guys, listen to me: If the fighters peel off they'll sweep along our flanks, then you start firing."

65 yards.

Sutton looked up.

He saw the details of the Junker—the rivets, the oil and exhaust stains, smears from oily hands, a few silver specks on the thin metal wings where the blue paint had chipped, the large black and white German crosses and the black swastikas on each of their tails. Sperrle's aircraft was so large now that it blocked the sunlight from *The Beast's* cockpit.

50 yards.

Sutton uttered one word: "Fire."

The Beast jarred.

Gunflashes lit the undersurface of the Junker and the hammering of .50-caliber machine guns deafened *The Beast's* crew through their headsets and the smell of cordite stung their nostrils. Rowe and Tutone worked their guns the way they would at gunnery school—smoothly, accurately, deftly.

Cannon shells pierced Baerenfaenger's fighter with a stunning ferocity that amazed

Tutone. He never shot anything this close, with such ease. Some of the rounds ricocheted, other passed clear through the wing roots. Leafy metal pieces ripped away.

"Oh my god!" said Baerenfaenger. The control stick jerked from his hand. The bullet-proof windscreen went snow-white and the sky vanished. Everything turned black and Baerenfaenger's forehead burned. There were several thumps and something rattled in the engine compartment. Dried mud that had accumulated on the floor suddenly exploded in a beige cloud and chunks of flooring blossomed up between his knees. The sixty-six-gallon center-line drop tank directly below his seat exploded and a tongue of flame plumed orange-blue in the slipstream. A flash of brilliant white light illuminated the cockpit. Tutone's four-second bursts had expelled twenty-two rounds of hot steel and high explosives. Four were effective. Baerenfaenger couldn't see, his eyes smeared with blood, but pilot instinct and rote precision took control. The Fw-190 performed a neat flick-roll and passed, flaming and bottomside-up, over the length of *The Beast's* fuselage.

Baerenfaenger's finger clutched the firing button and his 20mm Oerlikon cannons kicked off an eighteen-round burst as the fighter flew inverted. Calmly now, Baerenfaenger put his weight into the right rudder and yanked the stick over in the same direction. The nimble ship took the direction and began to roll over, its fuselage rattling and screaming. As he passed over *The Beast's* tail section, four release clips broke loose on the left cowling and it began flapping like a torn petal caught in a windstorm. For an instant, looking down as he hung from his seat, Baerenfaenger saw Tutone's eyes—they looked surprised, but no more than his.

The altimeter needle now revolved backward with frightening speed. Baerenfaenger's hands felt like heavy weights but he managed to reach up and check his parachute harness clip. Then he swabbed the blood from his eyes and was able to see clearly. A large piece of the .50-caliber shell had sliced across his forehead after impacting the flooring, cutting open the skin above his right eye. Flying level again, Baerenfaenger had control of his ship.

The ragged edge of vapor fire that trailed the center-line drop tank had extinguished itself. After the explosion, the fire lasted less than two seconds. The .50-caliber round that exploded the tank blew it into hundreds of pieces. The fuel had not been consumed yet and the blast ignited the fuel that had not yet leaked out. The remainder of the round, the size of a ragged marble, blew a cup-sized hole in the flooring and passed between Baerenfaenger's arms and legs. When it hit the bullet-proof windscreen most of the energy had been spend and it starred the glass then banged harmlessly around the cockpit before it fell under the instrument facia.

At the instant of explosion, Tutone erroneously thought he'd destroyed Baerenfaenger, so fierce and bright was the explosion. "I got him!" Tutone screamed. One second later Baerenfaenger was speeding past him, firing his cannons.

One of Baerenfaenger's HE shells slammed against the rear canopy framing of Kid Kiley's compartment. A slither of hot steel the length of a cigarette pierced the skin of his shoulder and he screamed. The metal hit with such force that he reacted violently and slammed his head against the top of the compartment, momentarily dazing himself. The wound burned and felt on fire, which it was. The area of impact on his flight jacket was smoking and he reached up and grabbed it and saw blood. Panic-stricken, his heart pounding, Kiley wanted to escape. He reached down and grabbed the emergency release handle on the hatch. He yanked it and gale-force wind from the slipstream tore it away. Then he looked out through the Plexiglass and saw Baerenfaenger's fighter. He forgot about bailing out and tried to grab the handles of his guns but couldn't move his right arm.

Rowe found it difficult firing into *Hauptmann* Prince Ritter von Woll's Focke-Wulf, trying to kill someone this close. He did it more for self-protection than any other reason. Rowe had fired a three-second burst and watched the fighter flutter like a wounded bird. Slowly, it rolled over onto the port wing. It seemed too still and flew too smoothly to be real, Rowe thought. He was mesmerized by the sight and didn't fire again. The Prince's fighter continued, wings vertical, hanging in the air, the undersurfaces facing the Junker's port wing. The Fw-190's flap motor had disintegrated, shattering a large hole through the triple webbing "I" beam adjacent to it. The explosion ripped away the double gun bay reinforcement. A second shell fragmented the aileron hinge bracket, blowing the control surface off the trailing edge of the fighter's wing. Without it now, the fighter began to roll.

As it slid down, curving left, Rowe came out of his fascination and fired again. His one-second burst splattered through fuselage section "C," going up through the bottom of the ship. The burst smashed the battery and the compass, exploded the oxygen bottle, and severed the tailwheel retracting cable.

The Prince's cockpit began to smoke from the fire in the center-line fuel tank, which was in the fuselage under his seat. The rubber seal at the aft edge had been damaged and caught fire. As the burning rubber dribbled into the tank, the fuel sloshing inside rose in temperature. After a few seconds, a large drop ignited the vapor and the tank

245

exploded, blowing metal, spark, and flames along the undersurface. The Prince was shocked, filled with horror. His ship was out of control, upside down now, curving away from the Junker he was to protect. He couldn't breathe and reached for the oxygen mask and sucked hard, but the air bottle had been rendered useless. Smoke and gas vapors made his eyes tear.

The Prince reached for the emergency handle near the canopy crank and pushed down. Normally this would cause an explosive charge to fire, ejecting the canopy into the slipstream where it would catch and fly off. But two of Rowe's shells had splattered under the rear of the canopy rails.

The Prince was trapped. The countryside was under his head. Trees and farmhouses spun, inverted. He watched them coming up, the cows and horses above, not below. The airspeed indicator revolved higher. Now the Prince's fighter was in a vertical dive and the controls were nonexistent. He pushed again on the emergency handle but the cartridge did not explode. Four knuckles were shattered and the metacarpus bone on the Prince's hand broke trying to beat his way through the moulded canopy. He had a girlfriend in Berlin, a beautiful woman waiting in Paris. The Prince was healthy and young, handsome and popular with his fellow pilots. His family had given him enough money to start his own business.

Why couldn't he live? With both hands flat against the peak of the canopy, the Prince screamed one word: "Damn!"

The Prince's fighter hit Monsieur Roche's farmhouse and scooped a hole ten feet deep and twenty-five feet wide. The largest section was the tail plane. The forward part of the fuselage hit the living room of the farmhouse dead-center and demolished the whole structure. Plaster and wood and broken bricks covered bed sheets, pots and sauce pans, and books. Dishes mixed with cables, chair legs with spars, fuel lines with carpeting. The BMW 801D-2 engine had cut a furrow from the farmhouse to the stone wall forty yards away. Pieces of the Roches mingled intimately with instruments and twisted wing panels. There was the stench of burnt chickens and hot carbon and hot metal tinkled like small cymbals.

A quarter-mile away the Prince hung limp from his parachute harness, which had been snagged by a tree. At the last possible moment he had pushed the emergency handle and the cartridge finally blasted the canopy loose. His hand was bleeding, swollen to twice its normal size. As he swung gently in the breeze he thought how wonderful it was to feel pain.

"Gunfire!" yelled Hund, his voice muffled by the fierce bangs of shells hammering around him, three consecutive hits wrenching the port wing upward. The primer caps ignited and the shells punched through the upper wing surfaces like bulbous mushrooms with razor-fine edges. Puffs of dust and clouds of burned gunpowder blossomed then vanished in the air. Hund dropped the plane through the shower of tracer rounds and flying metal until the wing, and the Junker's slipstream, gave it lateral stability and flattened it straight and level.

Hund did not doubt he'd been attacked from his seven o'clock low position, and now he was skillfully and calmly dropping the throttle back, using flaps, stalling the ship. He jerked the control column left, trying to get under and away from *The Beast's* guns. As he drifted past the bomber, momentarily pinned like a butterfly on a veil of blue, he glanced out at his torn wing—the top panel was tearing away, and the bulged access cover to the 20mm wing cannon had disappeared. Then he felt a quiver, a terrible shaking. The fabric-covered metal Frise-type aileron was missing.

Tutone's hits had blown away the riveted upper and lower skins from the hinge bracket. Hund no longer had control of his fighter. A second later, before Hund glanced away, Bush rolled his ball turret and framed the fighter dead-center in his crosshairs. At a distance of ninety-four feet, Bush triggered a long burst and watched the fighter shudder, blowing a dish-plate sized hole in the cockpit area. *Why did they have to choose us? Why couldn't they have done this to someone else? Why?*

Fear tightened Hund's rectum and bladder, and he felt his heart pumping blood faster and faster—now sugar-rich and thick with adrenaline. *My God, my heart is going to explode!* The controls were light! They were useless. *My heart is going to explode!* Fear strapped his throat and the blood coursing through his muscles and liver was releasing carbohydrates into his veins. *My heart!* Breaths were deeper, faster—the organism was on the verge of panic. Disaster. The brain was no longer logical, functioning, reading out options and possibilities, and incoming data was banal because—*Something . . . wrong with . . . my heart.*

Because every third shell from Bush's .50-caliber guns pierced armor with a reinforced point that burned at a temperature between 2000 and 3000 degrees centigrade for nearly one second. In two seconds, ten shells had been fired at Hund's ship. One was the lethal blow. It penetrated the cockpit through the tailplane radius arm aft of Hund's armor-plated seat, nicking the lipped edge and exploding on contact. The spent ignitor cap twirled like a dentist's drill at more than 12,000 revolutions per second, burring through Hund's chest with the efficiency of a blowtorch. The explosive impact wound the missle through his lower abdomen and chest. It exited above his right nipple after smashing two rib bones, blowing out a flesh hole the size of a grapefruit.

"My heart!" screamed Hund, gripping his bloody chest. *"God, help me, mother, mother!"*

His horror wasn't in his pain, which was minimal, but in the vision of his own blood: it had atomized into a cloud of fine red mist and bathed the entire cockpit, turning the sky's light a milky pink. He slumped over, cuddling his torn chest, and then his dead weight caused the fighter to dance like a crazy, palsied animal, passing under *The Beast's* tail section. One second later Hund's fighter disappeared in a ball of red fire.

Kid Kiley saw the even ripple of the shock wave and looked beyond the fighter's drifting debris and saw the last of the Eagles coming toward him with furious speed. August Baerenfaenger's Focke-Wulf was a flat slim speck flying straight and level. "Got one at six o'clock!" yelled Kiley into the interphone.

But Sutton didn't respond immediately. He was angling *The Beast* over toward Sperrle's diving Junkers, which was trailing a plume of oily smoke from the port engine. With hard right rudder and the control column pushed forward, *The Beast's* starboard wing had dipped low and the ship was swinging around in a tight arc.

"Hold it," Kiley shouted, "stop turning!"

The further *The Beast* turned, the greater the deflection was between Kiley's guns and Baerenfaenger's fighter.

"Holy Mother of God!" August Baerenfaenger said to himself. He didn't believe what he saw. The cowling, which had been flapping wildly in the slipstream, was wrenching loose. Now a weld clip had sheared and sped past the fuselage like a bullet. The cowling lifted up full, collapsed, banged down, then tore loose, smashing against the windscreen, tumbling slowly before it cracked against the rudder. At 250 MPH Baerenfaenger wondered if he was brave or just dumb. He tilted the ship over until the wings were perpendicular. This would be his last attack.

"Stop turning!"

No one minded Kiley's warning except Bush; their focus was on Sperrle's ship, which was about to disappear into a cloud bank. Bush spun his turret around and angled his guns toward Baerenfaenger, but it was too late. *The Beast* was at a forty-five-degree angle with the starboard wing dipped down. The Chief was concentrating on Sperrle's aircraft, and Tutone's guns were facing forward. From above now, Baerenfaenger's cannons were aimed at the top section of the bomber at a point just aft of Tutone's turret.

At a distance of five hundred yards, Baerenfaenger pressed the gun button.

A thump told Baerenfaenger that he'd passed through *The Beast's* slipstream. He was so close now that *The Beast's* wingtips were cut off in the gunsight. His cannons hammered away and the gunsmoke trailed behind. He watched the shells entering the bomber with a detached fascination. A newspaper-shaped piece blew off and sped toward him, growing larger with frightening speed until it crashed into the windscreen quarter panel turning it snow white. Baerenfaenger was unable to see. He pulled back on the control stick and climbed steeply, waiting for *The Beast's* cannon shells to hit his ship; but there was a sudden silence. He looked down at the instrument panel, at the fuel warning and pump indicator lights that were arranged vertically on the lower section. The fuel supply lights were flicking bright red. The ship was floating, without fuel, the nose falling over and the starboard wing dropping down.

In *The Beast,* the crew felt Baerenfaenger's shells thumping through the fuselage.

"What's that?" asked Sutton, finally recalling Kiley's warning. Two seconds later the attack was over.

The Chief, surprised, looked forward and saw the damage. "We've been hit," he said.

"This is Sutton, are you okay?"

"Yeah, okay. But there are four big holes on the port side of the ship. I'm walking up to take a look."

Kiley said, "I told you guys that we had one at six o'clock."

"Where is he?" asked Sutton.

"He broke off the attack and snapped over and disappeared. A piece of *The Beast* hit his canopy. I don't see him now."

At three thousand feet, below a thin cloud layer, Baerenfaenger was trying to make a quick decision—whether to bail out or try a crash landing. After looking at the fields and trees he reached for the emergency handle and pushed down. A small explosive charge behind a 14mm armor plate behind his head exploded and the canopy jerked up and blew off. Using the canopy rails, August Baerenfaenger pushed himself away from the seat and jumped. He waited four seconds then pulled the D-ring on his chute pack. A moment later he looked up and saw a perfect parachute slowing his descent.

Inside *The Beast* there was sudden shouting—a release of tension, the crew delighting in the sound of their own voices. They were alive; they had survived.

The Beast slid sideways now, still arcing around searching for Sperrle's aircraft, which seemed to have vanished. Sutton worked the controls, heard his crew's exhilaration, their shouts of victory. But through their noise, Tutone's sentence struck through, intact: "We missed Sperrle." Then, after a few moments, their voices dwindled like spent fireworks and there was cold silence.

"Sutton to Tutone."

"Yeah, boss, I'm still here."

"Did you get a good look at those fighters?"

"It was quick but, yeah, I did."

"Remember where we saw them last?"

Tutone thought for a second, then the vision came back like an old vivid photograph. "Yeah, I remember."

"Metz," said Sutton, "right after we got hit two of them pounced us."

"I wonder which two." Tutone said.

Sutton didn't answer. "Give me a heading for Bassingbourn," he told his navigator. "We're going home."

In the tail section Kid Kiley settled into his seat and closed his eyes but he did not sleep.